PUNAHOU BLUES

Also by Kirby Wright

Before the City

KIRBY WRIGHT

PUNAHOU BLUES

Lemon Shark Press

Published by Lemon Shark Press
San Diego, California
First Edition
ISBN 0974106712

"The Ring" and "Pakalaki Memories" appeared in slightly different
form in *Chaminade Literary Review*.

Printed in the United States of America
Set in Palatino
Designed by Lemon Shark Press
Cover Design by Holly Lewis

Lemon Shark Press
www.lemonsharkpress.com

For Darcy

ACKNOWLEDGMENTS

Much aloha to Maxine Hong Kingston, Frances Mayes, and Kurt Vonnegut, Jr. for inspiring me to become a writer. Heartfelt thanks to my posse for their encouraging words over the years: Chickie Lee Guillaume, Tom & Rici Conger, Jules Wright, Carol Fujishima, Allen Bernstein, Rooster, Loretta Petrie, Tom Henke, Alma, Ann Mesrobian, Lem, Karen Bumatai, Bonnie Judd, Jaimes Alsop, George & Jeannette Balint, Uilani, Jay McCullough, Joseph Bean, JeanPaul Jenack, Donna Mills, and in memory of Dave Donnelly and Robert Wright, Jr. I also want to acknowledge the nuns at Star of the Sea Elementary for a great education, especially Sister Ellen Saint Michael and Sister Mary Cornelius. Mahalo to my teachers Barbara Earle, Trudy Ellis, and Al Harrington at Punahou School. I am also grateful for two Arts Council Silicon Valley Fellowships, which gave me the time to complete this work.

CONTENTS

THE RING

It was Saturday morning and my mother was in the kitchen boiling an egg. I'd just finished a bowl of Sugar Pops at the dining room table across from my hapa haole father. He was reading *The Honolulu Advertiser* in his undershirt and khaki shorts. His glasses made his eyes look huge and his black, bushy eyebrows pushed down on the frames. He never shaved on weekends and that made him look tough.

My big brother Ben was watching *The Bugs Bunny Show* in the living room—he had his hands on the screen to warm them. His favorite show was *The Three Stooges* because he loved it when the Stooges beat each other up. Ben had my mother's blonde hair, green eyes, and fair complexion. He always burned at the beach. I rarely burned because I took after my father.

I was in first grade at Star of the Sea, a school run by nuns from Boston. My mother enjoyed going to PTO meetings so she could reminisce about her hometown. She'd been the first postwar Miss Massachusetts and met my father because the gods of pigskin fated it when Boston College upset Holy Cross on the last play of the game and she went to the Carlton Club to celebrate the BC victory. My father was there because he was attending Harvard on the GI Bill and law students got in free. He saw a tall blonde slow dancing with the Boston College quarterback and knew she was the one.

My mother's dream was to star in a Broadway musical. She'd given up on Ben and me becoming child stars after our first tap-dancing class at the Arthur Murray Dance Studio in downtown Honolulu. We'd ended up in a room full of girls, stage mothers, and a man wearing tights. Our tap shoes were still in their boxes when Ben told me to stand on my chair and click my flip-flops. I stood and clicked like a nut while Ben sang the *Felix the Cat* theme song. The man in tights kicked us out despite my mother's pleadings we were diamonds in the rough.

My mother carried in a plate of buttered toast and an egg perched in a ceramic cup—she placed her offering in front of my father. She wore a pink housedress and her beehive hairdo was petrified with hair spray. "How was your cereal, Jeffrey?" she asked me.

"Sugary."

"That will fill your tank with energy," she replied. She returned to the kitchen and ran water into the teapot.

My father cracked the eggshell by tapping it with his knife. He peeled off the top, carved out a sliver with his spoon, and put the sliver in his mouth. He chewed as he read. It was funny how my parents never ate breakfast together. She was his waitress. She'd stopped waiting on Ben and me because she said we were old enough to open cereal boxes and pour milk. I rarely started conversations with my father because I didn't want to say the wrong thing. He'd told my mother that he was "the king of the castle" and that his word was "the law of the land." Anything that threatened the smooth running of the household made him pupule. My mother prepared safe things for breakfast like boiled eggs, toast, and instant coffee. The teapot whistled in the kitchen.

"Who'd you kill?" I blurted.

"What?" my father asked through a mouthful of egg.

"In the war."

The teapot quit whistling and he raised his eyebrows. "What's this about the war?"

"Tom Wrigley's dad killed three Nazis."

"Oh, he did, did he?"

"Yeah. Shot 'em dead."

He took a bite of toast. "I didn't fight the Nazis," he said. "I fought the Japanese."

"Kill any?"

He told me about being an Army lieutenant during the Marshalls Campaign and firing his .3006 rifle at the enemy on the beachfront. His amtrac got stuck on the reef— soldiers waded through chest-deep water while the Japanese mowed them down. He saw owama nibbling the fingers of the dead. Howitzers drove the enemy back and, when he got on shore, the Japanese charged out of a coconut grove and engaged his platoon in hand-to-hand combat. A Japanese soldier bayoneted my father in the chest. My father pulled his Colt .45 and shot the soldier point blank. The Army sutured my father's wound and sent him back to fight. On Kwajalein, a colonel bumped him from an R & R flight to Honolulu—the plane went into a lazy turn and exploded in the ocean. They'd forgotten to take off the pylons and the wings were locked in the landing position. "If I'd been on that plane," my father told me, "you wouldn't be here."

"I'd be in Heaven."

"You'd be on the bottom of the deep blue sea."

"Was Uncle Bobby in the war?"

He scooped the bottom out of the egg and slid it in his mouth. "My brother was with the Seabees."

"Who'd he kill?"

My mother brought in a cup of Sanka for my father. "That's enough talk about killing," she said and stood there with her hands on her hips. Her face was shiny from the cream she applied every night before bed.

My father scanned the sports section. "Bobby spent the war building airfields for the Navy."

"Imagine," said my mother.

"Why'd he do that?" I asked toying with my spoon.

My father sipped his Sanka. "Bobby took the easy way out," he said, "as usual."

"Your brother sounds smart to me," said my mother.

"Bobby's a coward," my father replied. "You know,

Jeffrey, I have a Japanese flag from the Marshalls Campaign out in my footlocker."

"Can I see it?"

"I suppose."

My mother cleared the table. "I hope there isn't anything dangerous in that footlocker," she said.

My father stood up. "Only old letters from Carol."

"Who's Carol?" I asked.

"My girlfriend at UH."

"The one who left you," my mother said, "for that Air Force pilot."

Ben ran into the dining room. He was tall and lanky for a seven-year-old. "I wanna see that flag!"

"Let's go, boys," my father said and we followed him outside.

Ben nudged me in the ribs out in the driveway. "I'm the oldest," he told me.

"So?"

"So, so, suck your toe," he said, "all the way to Tokyo."

My father opened the storage room in back of the garage—an olive green footlocker had been pushed in the corner. He grabbed its leather handle and slid it away from the wall. The footlocker had PROPERTY OF THE US ARMY on its side and MAJOR NORMAN GILL on its lid. My father unlocked it, popped the metal clasps, and opened the lid. Ben and I peered in—a tray was packed with chrome and brass badges, ribbon bars, khaki and olive green side caps, and blue shoulder patches with red arrows.

Everything smelled like mothballs. Ben grabbed a handful of badges. I took some patches.

"How come these patches have arrows?" I asked.

"Those arrows point to the front line," my father replied. He lifted the tray out and placed it on the hood of his Olds. A bayonet and a square of white cloth were on the bottom of the footlocker. He picked up the cloth and spread out his arms—a crimson sun seemed to rise from his chest.

"I cops it," Ben said.

My father looked down at the flag. "See the blood?"

There were brown stains in the white fabric surrounding the sun.

"That's chocolate," Ben said.

My father laughed. "Blood doesn't stay red after twenty years."

"Whose blood is it?" I asked.

"The Japanese soldier carrying the flag."

"Where's he now?"

"Pushing up daisies," he answered and draped the flag over the car's hood.

My father rifled through a stack of letters while we rooted through the tray. The best thing wasn't the flag. Nothing from the war, including the bayonet, could match it. Ben found it in a buckskin marble bag—a gold band encrusted with diamonds. He turned it so the diamonds caught the light. "I cops this," said Ben.

"Gimmee that," my father said and took the ring. He examined it briefly before dropping it in his pocket.

"Whose ring was it?" asked Ben.

"Granny's."

"Who's Granny?" I asked.

My father grabbed the bayonet and slid the blade out of its sheath. "Your great grandmother."

"Is she still alive?" Ben asked.

"Granny died after the war."

"Mummy should have the ring," I decided.

My father ran a finger over the edge of the blade before sliding on the sheath. "I already gave her a ring," he said. He put the bayonet back and dropped in the tray. He let us have the flag, side caps, patches, and a handful of badges before closing the footlocker and shoving it back against the wall.

*   *   *

Ben and I divided up the badges and patches. We made a deal he'd keep the flag and I'd keep the side caps. I brought the side caps to school and distributed them to my friends at recess. We put the caps on our heads and I led a march from the convent over to the rectory through a field of kuku weeds and sour grass. Grasshoppers flew for cover. I found a dirt path skirting the field and that made the marching easier. We crossed paths with Father Keelan.

"Cub Scouts?" Keelan asked.

"We're in the Army now," I said.

"Thou Shalt Not Kill," he replied.

"We only kill bugs, Father."

Keelan saluted. "Well, carry on, men."

*   *   *

After school, Ben tied the flag to a bamboo pole and waved it in front of Violet, our cleaning lady. "Look at me," Ben said, "I'm Japanese!"

Violet put down her blue feather duster. "Dat flag from da war?"

"Yeah," Ben said. "It's got blood."

"That's not chocolate," I added.

"Like me wash?"

"Nope," Ben replied, "this blood belongs in the Bishop Museum."

Violet was the latest in a long line of cleaning ladies, women who worked all day Friday cleaning our house. My mother had thrown in the towel when it came to pleasing my father with her housekeeping abilities. Whenever he said everything was a mess and a disgrace to him as a professional man, my mother fired the cleaning lady and hired a new one. A cleaning lady from Osaka had called my mother a "lazy Irish cow." A Samoan cleaning lady had challenged my father to a fistfight when he accused her of goofing off.

My mother had heard about Violet from Mrs. McCormack, a fellow Bostonian and niece to the late Mayor Curley. "These Filipinos do windows," Mrs. McCormack had said. Violet took the bus from Pearl City every Friday and arrived at our house at the crack of dawn. My mother let her in through the back door. She was a tiny woman with brown skin and turtle eyes. She wore an apron with nozzles, sponges, and cleaning fluids sticking out of the pockets. Violet kept her eyes down whenever she spoke and walked with a limp. "The poor woman had polio," my mother whispered. Violet cleaned the bathrooms, made the beds, washed, ironed, vacuumed, and dusted. My mother didn't stick around to supervise; instead, she hustled down to Kahala Avenue and took the bus to Ala Moana Shopping Center.

Violet usually made it to my room after I got home from school. I felt bad seeing her wrestle the vacuum down our narrow hallway. I darted to my room, picked up my dirty clothes, and threw them in the hamper. I made the bed. It was as if Violet was my guest and I wanted her stay to be a pleasant one. I tossed toy soldiers into a big cardboard box and dragged my palm over the desk to clear it of dust.

"No need," Violet said from the doorway.

Ben charged around the house waving the flag. "Bonzai," he said, "bonzai!" He'd invented a history for the flag and played both parts—first, the Japanese commander waving the flag, then the Army sergeant who kills him.

"The commander can't die," I said.

"How come?"

"He's in charge of the flag."

"So?"

"If the flag falls, so does Japan."

Ben made a gun with his index finger and thumb and brought the barrel up to his forehead. "Right between the eyes," he said and squeezed off a round. He fell and his body convulsed on the living room floor. Sometimes

Ben fell where Violet was mopping and she had to mop around his convulsing body.

Ben organized the neighborhood kids into opposing armies and used the flag as the centerpiece for war games. The Asian boys didn't want to be on the side with the flag because that side had to lose after a fierce battle over a patch of mondo grass in our front yard. We hurled baby coconuts like hand grenades and shot each other with cap guns and air rifles. I was always on the side with the flag. I didn't mind. The Imperial Army would have been proud of the way I defended the Rising Sun on its bamboo pole. "Americans die!" I said and charged with my aluminum Samurai sword in one hand and the flag in the other. Ben and Larry Wong swung down off the hala tree and fired their rifles. I took a final swipe with my sword before collapsing on the mondo grass.

*   *   *

My father kept Granny's diamond ring on the top shelf of the medicine cabinet in his bathroom next to a blue jar of anti-itching cream. I saw it through the glass shelf whenever I slid the cabinet open for toothpaste. The ring haunted me. It promised no shallow glitter of rhinestones. The sparkling diamonds were mysterious and inviting. The ring had a voice and the voice said, "Take my diamonds." I resisted. I'd learned Thou Shalt Not Steal at school. One night I couldn't resist—I climbed up on the bathroom counter and grabbed the ring. The gold was cool to the touch. Colors moved through the rows of diamonds. The rows reminded me of the pineapple fields on Moloka'i. It was a tapered ring where the diamonds started out smaller on either edge of the band but grew in size toward the middle. I decided a diamond or two would be a great addition to my stash of brass bullet casings, Indian Head nickels, and steel pennies minted during the war. I remembered the Ten Commandments and put the ring back.

*   *   *

One Sunday after Mass, Ben and I walked to Piggly Wiggly with our mother. We followed her as she guided a shopping cart down the frozen food aisle. She loved pulling packages out of the freezer at home because she said it made cooking a breeze. She stopped at the TV Dinner section and filled our cart with Swanson's Fried Chicken and Salisbury Steak.

"How come you don't wear Granny's ring?" I asked her.

"I already have a nice ring."

"Granny's ring has fat diamonds," Ben said.

She pushed her cart toward the boxes of frozen vegetables. "I like a simple ring."

I looked at my mother's hand. Her ring had only specks of diamonds embedded in a silver band. Those weren't real diamonds.

After my father picked us up outside Piggly Wiggly and drove us home, I headed for his medicine cabinet. I plucked the ring off the shelf, took it into my room, and tried opening a tooth on a smaller setting with my fingernails. The gold was tough. I visited the kitchen and returned with a steak knife. I slipped the edge of the blade under a diamond. I pried and pried until the diamond popped free. I pried out a second. When I had three diamonds, I returned the ring to the shelf and closed the cabinet.

*   *   *

The diamonds went with me whenever I took a bath. I liked the feel of them under me, especially the sound they made squeaking against the tub in my mother's bathroom. I decided that, since nobody wore the ring, I might as well enjoy a few of the diamonds. I could always squeeze the diamonds back into their settings. As the weeks went by, I added more diamonds to my collection. I'd already worked through the small ones and was starting in on the mediums. I even popped out a big one—that looked obvious, but it looked less and less obvious the more that I mined. One early evening during my bath, I heard shoes pounding down the hallway. My father walked in loosening his tie as my mother placed fresh towels on the rack.

"Mary," my father said.

"Yes, Dear?"

The bubbles from my bubble bath were fading and you could see the blue bottom of the tub. It was like looking through a partially cloudy sky. Twenty diamonds sparkled on the bottom.

"Do you know anything about Granny's ring?"

"No, Dear."

"Someone busted the gold setting and stole the diamonds. Your Violet's a diamond thief."

"Violet wouldn't do that."

"She cleans my bathroom, doesn't she?"

"Why, yes."

"I'm going to ask her this Friday." He pulled off his tie and walked out.

My mother shook her head. "I wonder who took those diamonds?"

"I dunno," I answered. A diamond was rolling toward the drain and I dragged it back with my heel.

"I'm going to start the dinner, Jeffrey. You like lamb chops with mint jelly, don't you?"

"Yes, Mummy."

She placed my towel on the edge of the tub and left. I heard talking. The voices got louder. I figured I couldn't get blamed if nothing linked me to the crime. I herded the diamonds, pushed them to the rim of the closed drain, and reached for the lever that would flush them out.

"Finished?" my mother asked.

My heart pounded in my throat.

"When you're done, Jeffrey," she said, "you can set the table." She returned to the kitchen and started clanging pots and pans. You could measure my mother's mood by how loud she clanged—it was an average clang night. I thought about the diamonds. Why should I get rid of something I loved? Slippers slapped down the hallway. I flipped the lever and the drain made a waterspout. I heard the freezer door open and a hand digging for ice. I felt along the bottom of the tub, found two stray diamonds, and pushed them down. The drain gurgled. I dragged my hand over the bottom of the tub.

The evidence was gone.

*　　　*　　　*

It was Friday at dawn. The front door was open because my father liked it that way before a big trip. My suitcase was wedged against the door to prevent it from slamming. Ben and I were leaving for Moloka'i to spend the summer with our grandmother. Someone knocked at the back door and my mother opened it—Violet walked in carrying the crate of milk and juice the milkman had left. Violet set the crate on the counter and my mother offered her a cup of coffee. She asked for tea.

"I'll press charges," my father'd threatened the night before.

"Maybe the poor woman needs money for an operation," my mother had replied.

"I won't have a thief working for us, Mary."

"Well, I guess you're right."

Violet sat at the kitchen counter sipping tea from a Harvard mug. She pulled out a vanilla wafer from a paper bag and dipped it into the tea. I felt bad knowing she'd be accused of my crime. My father planned to come home for lunch and confront Violet. He wanted a half-day of work to wear her down so it would be easier for her to admit her guilt. I wanted to tell my father the truth but I didn't want to get whacked.

Ben charged into the living room swinging a suitcase. "I'm going to Moloka'i," he said in his singsong voice, "I'm going to Moloka'i." He plopped his suitcase next to mine.

Violet sipped her tea.

My mother put the milk and juice in the fridge. "The boys are visiting my mother-in-law," she explained.

"Good to visit tutu," said Violet.

My father walked in wearing a black suit. "The train's pulling out," he said and grabbed our suitcases.

My mother escorted Ben and me to the front door and followed us out to the garage. My father popped open the trunk of his Olds and moved boxes to one side.

"Have good time," Violet called from the doorway.

"We will," I said.

My mother opened the passenger door and watched us slide into the front seat. "Give Gramma my love," she said.

"You don't love her," Ben replied, "and she doesn't love you."

"That's enough," my father said loading in our suitcases. He kissed my mother goodbye, climbed in, and fired up the Olds.

I glanced over at the doorway as my father backed out—Violet had on her cleaning apron and she waved goodbye with her blue feather duster.

*   *   *

I sipped pineapple juice as our twin prop descended on the west end of Moloka'i. Ben chewed gum and blew bubbles in the window seat. The airport was built near a savannah of kiawe trees and lantana. Deer roamed the shallow gulches. This was going to be our third straight summer on what locals called "the Lonely Isle." It had become an annual tradition for our parents to send us away every June. My father banished us to Moloka'i because he wanted his mother to toughen us up. My mother said her blood pressure skyrocketed when we weren't in school so our leaving restored her health. "Absence makes the heart grow fonder," she claimed. My mother was not alone in her belief we were difficult children. None of the Star of the Sea mothers wanted to carpool with Ben and me because we either fought constantly or ganged up on their children. The only mother that lasted for more than two weeks had to gulp Valium. "First and last" applied to carpools as well as birthday parties. At our last pool party, Ben had practiced his swan dive off the roof while I was busy dunking the birthday boy's head.

Our plane landed on a strip of pockmarked asphalt and the wheels narrowly missed a mongoose scurrying across the tarmac. We taxied over to a bungalow surrounded by a cyclone fence. My grandmother stood behind the fence—she wore a lauhala hat with a wide brim, a palaka blouse, and blue jeans. Gramma had driven from Hale Kia, her ranch on the east end. She always left three hours before our scheduled arrival in case of a flat tire on her thirty-five mile trek over dirt, gravel, and asphalt. She was never in a good mood because she'd lost her patience waiting.

In the old days on Moloka'i, Gramma had earned a reputation as a clairvoyant. She could see people dying, babies being born, and ghosts. She fought for her life when an 'O'io Marcher choked her in a dream. Her jeep had once died outside a sacred kamani grove on a pitch-black night; she had pork in the jeep and, after she placed the meat on a stone in the grove, the jeep started. "Akua pololi," she'd told me, "hungry ghosts." The pineapple workers rode horses to Hale Kia to have her read their fortunes from a deck of playing cards. The men were worried about finding wives. They held black-and-white photos of picture brides during their readings, photos stained with the red dirt from the fields. It was funny how she made time for strangers yet gave Granny custody of her boys. Chipper, Gramma's third lover and first try at marriage, wanted nothing to do with raising the two sons she had out of wedlock.

The plane came to a rest beside the bungalow and a Hawaiian man pushed a stairway on wheels toward us. After a few minutes the stewardess opened the door and we followed the other passengers down the stairway.

"Race you," Ben said when we reached the asphalt.

We raced over the tarmac. Ben held a stack of pies in pink boxes. The boxes were tied together with pink string and they swung back and forth as he ran. We beat everyone to the bungalow.

"Watch those damn pies, Juicy!" Gramma scolded through the fence. Her nickname for Ben was "Juicy" because he could drink pitcher after pitcher of canned juice—she couldn't make it fast enough. She called me "Peanut" because of my size.

Ben darted through the open gate. Planters with white hibiscus were stationed around the bungalow. The dirt in the planters was full of cigarette butts and gum wrappers. Gramma snatched the pies from Ben.

"Minced and pumpkin," Ben said.

"Betta not be kapakahi," Gramma replied. She spoke a type of creole common on Moloka'i, a dialect interspersed with Hawaiian words. The more Hawaiian you spoke the more you were considered part of the aina. "How's li'l Peanut?" she asked.

"Fine," I answered.

Gramma offered us a cheek and we took turns kissing her. She smelled like baby powder. Her skin was white and her eyes slanted. Blue veins bulged out of the tops of her hands and her fingers were bent by arthritis. She was the same height as Violet but seemed taller because she looked you straight in the eye. Her serious nature reminded me of my father.

A Hawaiian woman wearing shorts and a Pau Hana Inn T-shirt approached us. "Oh, Brownie," she said, "these yoa mo'opunas?"

"Ae," Gramma said. "Norman's boys."

"Like two angels, no?"

"Christ, they're damn devils."

The woman stared at Ben and me accusingly. "Auwe," she said.

We claimed our suitcases and followed Gramma out into the parking lot. A pole flew the US flag on top and the Hawaiian flag below. We climbed into Gramma's red jeep and drove east toward Kaunakakai. She pulled over when we reached the pineapple fields. "Shoot yoa pickles," Gramma said.

"What about cops?" Ben asked.

"I'll toot to warn ya, Juicy."

I followed Ben out. Pineapple plants covered the flatlands and the foothills of Kualapuu. It seemed as if Moloka'i was one big field of pineapples. The plants were short and serrated leaves protected their fruit. Most of the pineapples were small and green but Ben had the pineapple eye. He found a row of ripe ones and waved me over. I reached through the sharp leaves, grabbed the orange globe of fruit, and spun it to separate it from the plant. I heard a plane and looked up—it was the same one that had brought us. I watched its shadow move through the fields like a ghost.

*   *   *

That first night at Hale Kia, Gramma served pineapple shrimp over rice at the big koa table in the living room. The table was wedged against a picture frame window so Gramma could eat and watch her ranch at the same time. Her lauhala hat rested on the far corner of the table but she still had on her palaka shirt and jeans. Outside on the glass, geckos hunted moths and flying beetles. Gramma put down her fork and studied the window. "Ya boys see sumpthin' inside those damn lizards?"

The light from the lamp cut through the geckos' bodies and highlighted veins and yellow egg sacks.

"See what?" Ben asked.

"Eggs."

"No."

"Can you see eggs, Peanut?" Gramma asked.

Ben kicked me under the table.

"No," I lied.

"Yoa Gramma must have this X-ray vision."

Ben nodded. "Like Superman."

The phone rang in the kitchen and she took her eyes off the geckos. "Pesty," she said and left the table. She picked up the receiver and mumbled a greeting. "Ae," she said, "right on time. What?"

Ben left the table and snuck over to the entrance of the kitchen. He stuck his hands in the pockets of his jeans. "She's talking to Daddy," he whispered.

"About what?"

"Granny's ring."

"Sounds fishy to me, Normy," Gramma said and hung up. Ben beat her back to the table.

Gramma entered the room and stared at us. A minute passed and she was still staring.

"What's wrong, Gramma?" I asked.

"Sumpthin' terrible," she replied. "This lady yoa big horse mutha hired, what's her name?"

"Violet," Ben said.

"Yoa fatha says Violet pulled diamonds outta my mutha's weddin' ring. Why didn't ya keeds keep an eye on her?"

"Violet works when we're at school," Ben answered.

"Whea's that big horse durin' all this malarkey?"

I raised my fork. "Shopping at Ala Moana."

"Foa the luva Pete," Gramma said and sat back down. She scratched a wooden match against the edge of her Lancer's matchbox and lit a Chesterfield.

Three geckos on the window surrounded a beetle and took turns snapping at it. The beetle flew off and settled on a tree fern in the garden. The geckos chirped like birds.

"I gotta mana'o ya keeds know who stole those diamonds."

"Violet," Ben said.

"Or a cat burglar," I blurted.

Ben nodded. "Could even be the milkman."

"I know one thing foa certain," Gramma said after blowing smoke out of her nose.

"What?" Ben asked.

"Diamonds don't march off by their bloody selves."

*   *   *

I was wide-awake between Gramma and Ben on the big pune'e bed we shared. Gramma was snoring. A half-moon glared down and the room was alive with shadows. The shadows were from the ferns and trees outside but they seemed to have human faces. The faces shook when the wind blew and it looked as though they were yelling. A screen door led to a lanai. The storm windows were open and waves crashed on the beach. A Big Ben alarm clock sat on the coffee table. The ticking kept pace with my heart. The fluorescent hands said it was three. A poi dog named Skippy was lying beside the table—he growled whenever I looked down at him.

Gramma had told me she dreamt of her boys before meeting their fathers. She had visions warning of danger and drank red eye to ease her nerves. That brought the

make moe'uhane—death dreams. Sleep carried her to the
Aina of the Dead, where the living walked arm-in-arm with
the deceased. She visited a luau where her mother danced
for King Kamehameha on the shore of an ocean as calm as
a millpond. The beach was covered with opihi—when she
got closer, she saw they weren't opihi at all but human
mouths. They warned her to leave. The make moe'uhane
gave Gramma a reputation as a kahuna, a witch who could
kill with a curse.

Gramma quit snoring. She pulled off her blankets
and walked over to the screen door. "Who did it?" she
asked. "Who stole yoa diamonds?"

The wind howled and the faces on the walls shook.
A mysterious whisper, deep and gravelly, came from the
other side of the screen. Next came a hissing sound. A
cold wind blew through the room. Skippy stood on his
haunches and whined. Ben tossed and turned beside me.

"Ae," Gramma said, "that's it." She left the screen
door and switched on the lights. She wore blue long johns.

Skippy growled at me from the edge of the pune'e
and I pulled the covers over my face.

"Ya pests get up!"

I lowered the covers and shielded my eyes with my
hand.

"What time is it, Gramma?" Ben asked.

"Time to tell the bloody truth."

"Huh?" I asked.

"Ya keeds know sumpthin'."

"Do not," Ben said rubbing his eyes.

Gramma stood over us—her mouth had caved in. Then I remembered she always took out her dentures before bed. The waves rolled up the beach and crashed.

"I'm going back to sleep," Ben said.

"Oh, no, yoa not."

"How come?"

"I'm gettin' to the bottom of this ring business, one way or anotha."

My face felt hot. My cheeks ached trying to keep a straight face. My heart pounded in my chest.

Gramma stared at me. "Tell me ya didn't do it, Peanut," she said, "and may God strike ya dead if yoa lyin'."

"He'll kill me?"

"If yoa tellin' stories."

I looked over at Ben. He looked away. I remembered the Ten Commandments. "It wasn't Violet," I admitted.

"Ya did it, Peanut."

"Yes."

"And ya had a helpa."

"No."

Gramma looked at Ben. "Whacha lookin' so funny foa, Juicy?"

"I did it too."

"Peanut and Juicy did it," Gramma said, "togetha."

Ben shook his head. "Alone."

"Ridiculous," Gramma said. "Ya musta known yoa brutha was pullin' diamonds outta the same damn ring."

"No."

"Whea'd ya keeds put the bloody diamonds?"

"Down the drain," I said.

Gramma's eyes bugged out. "What?"

"Mine are gone too," Ben said.

"Yoa both lyin'."

But we weren't. Ben and I had attacked the ring separately, without the other knowing. Ben admitted he broke the gold band with a screwdriver trying to free the biggest diamond.

"Whacha do with yoa diamonds, Juicy?" Gramma asked.

"I liked watching them sparkle in the water."

"Christ," she said, "well whea are they now?"

"I put them in the kitchen sink and they all washed down."

Gramma sat on the edge of the pune'e and shook her head. "I'll be a monkey's uncle," she said.

*   *   *

The next night, after Gramma phoned our father and told him the truth, Ben peed in his sleep. Gramma spanked him in the morning with her bamboo stick. She spanked me too. She never forgave us for what we'd done. I never forgave myself for letting Violet take the blame. My father had accused Violet of stealing. She'd insisted she was innocent and he threatened to call the police. He'd fired her when she continued to plead innocence. My mother asked Violet to come back after finding out we were the culprits. She refused. The day we returned to Honolulu, our father told us on the drive home we were going to learn our lessons. He marched Ben and me to our rooms, had us take off our clothes, and beat us with his belt.

*   *   *

Ben and I tried to make sense out of what we'd done. It was strange how all the diamonds went down the drain.

"Granny made us do it," Ben said.

"Why?" I asked.

"She didn't want Mummy getting her ring."

"What's wrong with that?"

"Mummy's not Hawaiian."

Ben believed the ghost of our great grandmother didn't want her ring on a haole woman's finger so she had us destroy it. I told Ben about hearing Gramma talk through the screen door. Ben said she was talking to Granny's ghost and that Granny had us do her dirty work because we were young and she could exert power over us. It made me think the dead are watching and have the power to change our lives. But if that was true, I wondered how Granny felt knowing my father had blamed an innocent woman.

*   *   *

I saw Violet once more. It happened years later when I was riding the bus home from school. I was daydreaming and passed my stop on Kahala Avenue. I yanked the cord and the bus pulled over. I marched down the stairs and Violet stood at the curb—her blue feather duster was sticking out of her purse and she was holding a green bus ticket. I wanted to say something, to apologize. I couldn't find the words. She kept her eyes to the ground and waited for me to get off before getting on. The door closed. Violet limped to the back of the bus. The engine groaned and the bus lurched forward. A black cloud spewed and I breathed in the fumes.

I stood at the curb and watched the bus disappear around Diamond Head.

PAKALAKI MEMORIES

Gramma rarely visited us on Oahu. "Pakalaki memories," she said. Returning to the island of her youth made her feel defeated because it was where two men had deserted her. One of those men, a blond Englishman named Wilkins, would have been my grandfather. His parents had financed his travels during the Great War so he wouldn't die fighting for his country. Wilkins met my grandmother at Ala Park in Honolulu, where she was a chorus girl for the Ziegfield Follies. He handed her a bouquet of roses when she hopped off the stage and he told her she was the most beautiful girl he'd ever seen. They were engaged two weeks later. But my grandmother's beauty was not enough to keep Wilkins in the islands—when he found out she was pregnant, he was on the next steamer bound for San Francisco. My father was born manuahi the first day of world peace.

The second man who left Gramma was Danford, a

longshoreman she'd met at her mother's birthday party in
Kapiolani Park. She had a baby but Danford still dated
her. When Danford got her pregnant, he told her he wasn't
going to marry a girl who already had a son out of wedlock.

*   *   *

Whenever Gramma traveled to Oahu, she preferred
to stay with my father's half-brother Bobby in Kaneohe
rather than with us in Kahala. Ben and I were partly to
blame. We'd bolt the front door whenever guests were
expected and only opened it for those who brought
presents. We watched from behind the louvered window
on Gramma's first visit—she got out of the Olds and headed
for the house.

"Wha'd ya bring me," we asked her, "wha'd ya bring
me?"

Gramma tested the doorknob. "Open the bloody
doah."

"Wha'd ya bring me?"

"I brought ya keeds a big stick."

Ben and I always exhausted Gramma's patience
during our summers on Moloka'i. If we got her mad when
she visited Honolulu, she'd pull a bamboo stick out of her
suitcase and whack us. My mother gave her the maid's
room, a small room with a bath on the street side of the
house. Gramma hated the maid's room because it
overlooked the sidewalk. She said sidewalks gave puhi'us
an excuse to peek in while she was changing. She didn't
appreciate "complete strangas" whizzing by in cars.
Gramma told me our house was built kapakahi because

only one door faced north and none faced south—that meant ghosts marching down from the mountains at night to go fishing could enter but couldn't get out. She said she heard ghosts searching the cupboards for food at midnight.

"Bet it was my father," I told her.

She shook her head.

"Maybe it was my mother."

"Christ," she said, "that big horse sleeps like a log."

Gramma said she was sure we had ghosts because she couldn't see any light from the kitchen spilling under her door. "Akua don't need light," she explained. I started thinking our house was a ghost trap and that thousands of ghosts were congregating in the hall, up in the attic, and under my bed. I slept with rosary beads around my neck— I jerked my head during a nightmare and the beads nearly choked me.

My mother made Gramma feel less than welcome in Kahala. She'd never forgiven her for destroying our pink suits and hurling our baskets into a pineapple field on an Easter visit. She resented Gramma for always forgetting her birthday. My mother had never learned how to make a lei and, if my father suggested ordering one for Gramma, she told him plenty of leis were on sale at the airport. When it came to her mother-in-law, my mother believed in the adage: "Familiarity breeds contempt." Gramma got the hint. Bobby began picking her up at the airport and taking her to his home in Kaneohe.

My father didn't like his half-brother entertaining their mother on the other side of the island. There'd been bad blood between them since they were kids because my father believed Bobby was the favorite. My father insisted on paying for her room at the Young Hotel in downtown Honolulu, a stone's throw from his law office.

"Oh, Normy," Gramma said, "that's big money."

"Nonsense," my father replied.

My mother nodded. "Now you have your privacy, Mother Daniels."

My father had decided on the Young Hotel because of Gramma's weakness for sweets. The hotel boasted the best bakery on Oahu. He also figured she had a nostalgic interest in that hotel because she'd jitterbugged with Alan Ladd in its ballroom. Despite the bakery and the memories, Gramma was leery about sleeping alone in a city she considered the crime center of the Pacific. She never ventured out by herself. One night a drunk sailor banged on her door and begged "Lucky Linda" to come out. Gramma buzzed room service and ordered a butcher knife. Room service refused. She phoned HPD and got the sailor arrested. After that trauma, my father made sure Gramma got a room with two beds and had Ben and me take turns spending the night with her. When it was my turn, I realized she wasn't meant for hotels. She was meant to be talking story in a kama'aina home, not stuck in a place full of malahinis. She told me she could hear noises through the walls and claimed people were "monkeyin' " with one another.

"Are you sure they're monkeying?" I asked.

"Screamin' and bangin' to beat the band."

"Really?"

"Just goin' it," she said.

Gramma's biggest fear was that she'd fall asleep smoking in bed and burn the hotel to the ground. She was so worried about fires that she kept a small extinguisher in her suitcase. She insisted on staying in the same room on the second floor because it was above the sidewalk and had a handy escape ladder. Gramma's room also had a view of Bishop Tower, my father's building. She said she could look out anytime and see him hard at work in his office. Occasionally, Gramma ordered room service. If I was over and she didn't finish something on her plate, I'd toss it out the window when she wasn't looking. Once I splattered a truck's windshield with Eggs Florentine. Gramma didn't believe in giving tips so she earned a reputation as a skinflint. "Okole kala," our waiter whispered to the bus boy after our Saturday breakfast of macadamia nut waffles in the coffee shop.

"I wanna visit my mutha's grave," she said after paying at the register.

"Granny?" I asked.

She grabbed a handful of peppermint candies from a glass jar next to the register. "The one ya stole diamonds from," she said dropping the candies into her purse.

"Granny made me do it," I told Gramma.

"Ya bloody thief."

Gramma never let you forget a crime. But my criminal past wasn't enough to deny a visit to the bakery. The aroma of pastries wafted through the lobby as we walked across a black-and-white tiled floor. Gramma told me to stay on the white ones for good luck. A huge air conditioner blew out blasts of arctic air. Glass cases were loaded with eclairs, glistening bear claws, and cheese Danishes with swirls of apricot and peach. A haole baker in a chef's hat brought out a pan of poha cookies. Haupia, guava, and Black Forest cakes beckoned inside rotating displays. A special section featured mint and rocky road brownies. The rocky roads were crammed with walnuts and had a layer of marshmallow below the fudge topping. The mints had a green layer.

"Let's get sumpthin' foa Juicy," Gramma suggested. "What's he ono for?"

"A dozen mint brownies."

"He can have one," she said, "and that's plenny."

"Ben likes eclairs too."

"Christ," she said, "yoa brutha's a damn hog."

"May I help you?" asked the baker.

"Whacha want, Peanut?"

"An eclair."

"Two eclairs and one of those mint brownies," Gramma told the baker. She opened a coin purse and placed a half-dollar on the stainless steel counter. The baker told her she was a half-dollar short. She said, " 'Scuse me," and pulled out another.

We took the stairway back to the room because Gramma was worried about taking elevators after seeing a cable snap on an episode of *Perry Mason*. We polished off the eclairs and she phoned my father at home and talked him into visiting the cemetery. It wasn't easy because I heard him yelling through the phone. He always got mad whenever she suggested something that wasn't on his agenda. She put the receiver down and wiped away a tear.

"Are you okay, Gramma?" I asked.

She regained her composure and said, "Ae." She opened her compact and dabbed rouge on her cheeks.

*   *   *

I waited with Gramma out in front of the hotel. A family walked by in matching Aloha print muumuus and shirts. I swung the paper bag that held Ben's brownie. A Filipino bellhop asked Gramma if she needed a cab. She told him she was a kama'aina and that her son was a big time attorney with an Olds.

It was strange seeing my grandmother in something besides ranch clothes. Instead of her usual jeans and palaka blouse, she wore a dress with an orchid print. Instead of cowboy boots, she wore sandals with one-inch heels. Gramma had a strand of champagne-colored pearls around her neck that she'd bought on sale at Kaunakakai Drugs. She still wore a lauhala hat, but she considered this one more sophisticated because it had a fine weave and a narrow brim. She held her purse with both hands and shifted her weight from one sandal to the other as we waited at the curb. Gramma seemed upset, as if she was worried about doing or saying the wrong thing in a city full of businessmen and criminals. She had applied her rouge unevenly—one cheek made it appear she was blushing and the other had only a hint of pink. Red lipstick caked her thin lips. Her eyeliner highlighted the slant of her eyes.

Out on Bishop Street, the lanes were jammed with traffic. A bus belched exhaust. A traffic light next to the Hob Nob Restaurant turned red and boys jogged along the median strip selling *The Honolulu Advertiser*. "Pay-pah," they said, "Hanalulu Advatizah!"

Gramma watched the boys. "These Portagee keeds got moah guts than my mo'opunas."

"Do not," I said.

"What grade ya in now, Peanut?"

"Fourth."

The light turned green and Gramma watched the boys dodge traffic. "That big horse spoiled ya."

I tossed the bag with the brownie up in the air and caught it.

"Christ," Gramma said, "that damn brownie'll be busticated by the time yoa brutha gets it."

I tossed the bag again, tried my one-hand catch, and fumbled the bag on the sidewalk.

"Foa the luva Pete," Gramma said.

The Olds pulled up but my mother wasn't in the car. Ben was in the back seat—he made the "kiss my ass" sign at me through the side window and pressed his lips to the glass. He wore jeans and a T-shirt like me.

The bellhop opened the passenger door. "Have one shakadelic day," he told Gramma.

"Ya not gettin' a tip," she answered.

I climbed in back with Ben and Gramma slid into the front seat. The bellhop slammed the door.

My father sped down Bishop Street toward the wharf. He wore his horn-rimmed glasses like battle gear and had on his grouchy face. He told Gramma he'd made reservations at the Kahala Hilton for lunch.

Ben punched me in the arm. "Wha'd Gramma buy you?" he asked.

"Chocolate eclairs and mint brownies."

"Fatso."

"Where am I fat?" I asked. "I dare you to show me where I'm fat."

"You're fat all over, including the brain."

I handed him the bag. "Feed your face."

He opened the bag and grabbed the brownie. "It's my turn with Gramma tonight," he said and gobbled the brownie.

My father took the Waikiki way back because he wanted to point out all the hotels he'd drawn up contracts for. "The Ilikai wouldn't exist if it wasn't for me," he said. Gramma nodded and said how proud she was of Bobby managing the Queen's Surf nightclub. My father ran two yellow lights on Kalakaua Avenue. He braked for a third only because a policeman monitored the intersection. Tourists streamed over the crosswalk. My father looked at his watch. He seemed aggravated by Gramma's presence, as though she should be back on Moloka'i taking care of Hale Kia instead of wasting time in Honolulu. He'd already called her a kua'aina for coming off the plane wearing a fern-and-berry wreath around the crown of her hat.

Gramma rolled down her window, stuck a

Chesterfield on the end of a long chrome holder, and lit it with one of her Lancer's matches. She studied the tourists on the sidewalk and flicked ashes out the open window. "Damn puhi'us," she said.

We were heading for Diamond Head Memorial Park. I'd visited it once before with my father and Ben. My mother had come too but waited in the car while we searched for Granny's grave; she'd told me Granny had died three months before my father returned from Harvard. We'd widened our search but my father gave up and placed his carnations on a stranger's tombstone.

"Show people you love 'em while they're still alive," he'd said on the drive home.

"Death is so final," my mother'd said.

"When will I die?" I'd asked.

"When the cow jumps over the moon," my father had answered.

We stopped at No Ka Oi Flowers in Kapahulu, where Gramma bought red torch ginger and a pikake lei. The ginger had long thick stems and waxy red blossoms. Gramma purchased the pikake because it had been the flower Granny liked best. She'd always promised to send Granny money for raising my father and his brother but there was never anything extra because jobs on Moloka'i were scarce. Gramma was never on good terms with her mother, especially after sneaking out of the house to make love to Wilkins. Still, Granny kept a picture of the Englishman on her bureau in the hopes he would return. Although Granny had admired her daughter's fierce independence, she was disappointed in her for always ending up with the wrong men.

My father turned down Monsarrat Avenue. He didn't believe in God or life after death. "When you're dead," he'd said, "you're dead." He never went to Mass with us, even at Easter and Christmas. He drove up an incline skirting the northern side of the volcano. The slopes were fuzzy with bright green brush. We approached the only Dairy Queen in east Honolulu.

"I wanna chocolate dip!" Ben said. His lips and the corners of his mouth were outlined with fudge from the brownie.

"A who?" Gramma asked Ben.

"Dairy Queen."

"That's not real ice cream," my father said.

"I still want one."

"Kulikuli," Gramma scolded, "ya damn pest."

We turned left on 18th Avenue and hung a right at the entrance to Diamond Head Memorial Park. My father pulled over beside an office building shaded by a golden shower tree. Gramma swung her door open and climbed out. Ben pushed her seat forward and I followed him over a driveway dusted with small yellow petals.

"Don't go far," my father told us.

"We'll look for Granny," said Ben.

"No funny business," Gramma said.

My father and Gramma headed for the cemetery office. She looked tiny walking beside him. He opened the office door and they disappeared inside.

The cemetery was on the northeastern side of the crater, the side tourists rarely see. Clouds drifted across the sky. The park's plumeria trees were loaded with blossoms and dirt was mounded around open graves. The tombstones were massive: Chinese and Japanese symbols were carved on some of the faces and one had a portrait of a cat. A mynah bird landed on a marble slab. An end loader moaned on the east side of the cemetery and the American flag hung limp on a pole next to a bone-white mausoleum. A Chinese couple stood beside a headstone. The stone came up to the man's chest and he hugged it as if it was a person. Clouds moved over the sun.

Ben tagged me. "You're it!"

I chased him through the rows. "Don't step on the graves," I warned.

Ben stood behind the trunk of a plumeria tree. Next to him was a grave marked by a green sundial that had IN SILENCE I SPEAK engraved on the dial. "What's wrong with stepping on graves?" he asked.

"If you do, their ghosts will kill you."

"Who says?"

"Gramma."

"She's bugs." He ran out from behind the tree and jumped on a bronze tombstone shaped like an open book. He danced on the bronze pages in his Keds. "Kill me, kill me," he begged, "I dare you, I double dare you!"

I saw my father and Gramma heading across the lawn. Instead of walking with her, he walked in front. She was having trouble keeping up in her heels. A strap hung off one shoulder and her purse swung back and forth like a canteen.

Ben said safe base was a black tombstone with offerings of oranges and incense sticks. The incense had burned away and fruit flies camped on the oranges. I tagged him and reached safe base. Ben changed his mind about the headstone being safe and chased me around it. I accidentally kicked an orange and it rolled down the row of graves.

"Cut that out," my father said.

"No respect," Gramma said shaking her head.

My father unfolded a map and pointed to an X made in pencil. "Thirty-three graves makai of the curb," he said.

"Which way's makai?" Ben asked.

"Toward the sea."

Ben ran to the curb and started counting. When he reached thirty-three, he pointed down at a grave marked by a small rectangle of pinkish-gray granite. The granite was laid flat on the earth and it said:

GRANNY DEAR
Catarina Punawai Gill
Apr. 16, 1875—Jan. 8, 1949

HER MEMORIES WILL LIVE FOREVER

"How come it's not bigger?" I asked.

My father put his hands in his pockets. "She couldn't afford it."

"Can't we buy her a bigger one?"

"It's too late now," he said and walked back to the car to get the flowers.

"Ya keeds help out," Gramma said.

Ben and I helped Gramma pull out the grass and kuku weeds growing over the granite. I spotted a sunken plastic tube meant for flowers. The tube was dry but Ben found an empty soda can and filled it at a drinking fountain next to a statue of the crucified Jesus. He poured water into the tube. My father returned and I helped Gramma wedge in the stems of the torch ginger. She stood up, took off her hat, and mumbled in Hawaiian. I wasn't sure what she was saying but her voice was soft and sad. My father kept his eyes on the crater.

Mist began to fall.

"Let's go, Mother."

"Just anotha minute, Normy." She opened her purse and pulled out the pikake lei. She spread the blossoms so that they framed the granite.

My father looked at his watch. "Cheesus," he said, "we've been here all morning."

But it wasn't all morning. It wasn't even half-an-hour. My father reminded Gramma about his reservations and hustled us back to the car. We drove over to Aukai Avenue to get my mother and Gramma seemed sad. She took off her hat and didn't light up. "Don't bury me, Normy," she said.

"What?" my father asked.

"I don't wanna grave."

"How can you not have a grave?" Ben asked.

"I wanna be ashes."

"Then I can't visit you," I said.

"I don't want ya too, Peanut."

"How come?"

"Waste of time rememberin' me," she said.

*   *   *

We drove Gramma to the airport the next day. She rode between my parents in the front seat. Ben was in back with me. I cranked open the side window for air. Gramma wore a black dress with white stripes. She had on a white fedora with a black band. The hat was cocked to one side and it reminded me of the gangster hats in *The Untouchables*. Instead of pearls, she wore the plumeria lei I'd made her.

Ben had spent the night with Gramma but he told me she hadn't taken him to the bakery. She claimed she wasn't ono for sweets. When he said he was, Gramma told him the combination of eating pastries and drinking juice would turn his urine "acidy." She said the acid would eat pukas through his bladder and kill him. He told her he still wanted an eclair and was willing to risk death. She told him to pa'a his waha.

My father took Nimitz Highway to the airport and drove past the lei stands. He said Bobby had just been fired as night manager of Queen's Surf for drinking on the job.

"My Bobby can hold his liquor," Gramma said.

"Not this time," my father replied.

"I'm goin' to call Bobby and find out direct."

"Don't you believe me, Mother?"

" 'Course I believe ya, Normy."

"Let's face it," he said, "Bobby's a lush."

"Maybe the poor man can get some help," my mother suggested.

My father frowned. "He'll never change."

We waited with Gramma at the terminal. The day was hot and time dragged. We talked about Hale Kia's tides, the horses, and whether gardenias were blooming outside her mountain house. My father kept looking at his watch. Gramma lit a cigarette and sucked at it through her chrome holder. The plumeria on her lei were turning brown. Finally it was time to board. Gramma crossed the tarmac and took the steps up to the plane. We waited for her to wave to us when she reached the top step, the way she always did when she was leaving Honolulu.

She boarded without looking back.

PUNAHOU DAYS

It was Labor Day and my parents were admiring a Plymouth Barracuda parked in our driveway. It was a white two-door with chrome bumpers, turquoise racing stripes running fender to fender, and a blue vinyl interior. The plan had been to buy my mother a Valiant for basic transportation but she'd fallen in love with the Barracuda at Aloha Motors. "I'm glad you didn't settle for a Valiant, Mary," Mrs. McCormack had told my mother over the phone, "that's what all the little old ladies drive."

Ben was a week away from becoming a teenager. He swung open the car door and hopped into the driver's seat. He gripped the steering wheel, twisted it back and forth, and examined all the gauges on the dash. "Bitchin," he said fiddling with the radio knobs, "FM!"

"You never listen to FM, Juicy," I said.

"I will now, Peanut," Ben replied. "Bet Mom's Barracuda could beat Dad's Cutlass."

"Do you really think so?" my mother asked.

"Ha," my father said, "that's like saying a quarter horse could beat a thoroughbred." His expression waffled between pride and remorse. He was glad he could give my mother what she wanted but he seemed upset about the purchase, as though a good salesman had gotten the best of him. Once he'd nearly beefed a Samoan for overcharging him on a tree-trimming job. He kicked a tire and handed my mother a set of keys. "Now you have your independence," he told her.

"Well, Dear," she said, "isn't it about time?"

"Just don't forget my Miller High Life."

The keys to the Barracuda became the symbol of my mother's newfound freedom. She sang along to songs by Karen Carpenter and Helen Reddy while driving around Kahala wearing wigs, clip-on earrings, and glossy red lipstick. She kept her keys on a chain with a big brass "M."

"Why so big?" I asked her.

"So I never lose them."

I had mixed emotions about the Barracuda because I wanted a station wagon like the family in *The Brady Bunch*. I wanted to go steady with someone like Marcia or Jan, girls who dressed mod and spoke cool. My new school was full of girls like Marcia and Jan. I'd just started seventh grade at Punahou, a private institution established by Protestant missionaries in the 1800s. My father had attended Saint Louis, a rival Jesuit school near his childhood home in Kaimuki.

Ben and I had taken the entrance exam for Punahou

and my essay on the meaning of living in a glass house and not throwing stones impressed the admissions committee enough to give me the green light. Ben's essay wasn't as well received because he wrote about gunning down anyone who came within one hundred yards of his glass house. The committee said he could attend only if he stayed back. My father agreed and Ben was forced to repeat seventh grade. Punahou's strict admission policy, coupled with my father's desire to place his sons in what he considered the top local school, put Ben and me into head-to-head competition. My father examined us for flaws before the school year began. He thought of us as saplings and believed we would grow straight and strong if he applied splints early. He decided Ben had a severe case of pigeon-toes after examining his footprints in the sand.

"Ben walks like a blahlah," my father told me.

"Good runners are pigeon-toed," I said.

"Ben's the slowest kid in Honolulu."

My father bought Ben special shoes to fix his stride. He sent Ben to an orthodontist to fix his teeth and on to an optometrist to correct his vision. Ben had a mouthful of wire on the first day of school, headgear for his overbite, horn-rimmed glasses like my father's, and black shoes as heavy as combat boots. He was gangly and that accentuated the gear even more. It was as though Ben was going off to war, not school.

"I look like a geek," Ben said on our first drive to Punahou in our father's new blue Olds Cutlass.

"You'll thank me later," my father said.

"Can I have braces?" I asked from the back seat.

My father looked at me through the rearview mirror. "Nothing wrong with your teeth, Jeffrey."

"They're kapakahi."

"Quit speaking Hawaiian."

We merged onto the H-1 Freeway from the Waialae onramp and my father sped in the fast lane. Glenn Campbell sang "Wichita Lineman" on the radio as we traveled between the mountains to the north and the hotels in Waikiki to the south.

My father signaled with his blinker and took the Wilder Avenue exit. "Wish I coulda gone to Punahou," he said.

"What was wrong with Saint Louis?" Ben asked.

"Nothing. But Punahou grads run this island. All the best doctors and attorneys went there and so did most of the leaders in the business community. You boys should know it's very prestigious to graduate from Punahou because it's so hard to get into."

"Did you ever take the entrance exam?" I asked.

"There was no reason to," he answered, "my grandmother couldn't afford it." The date palms of Punahou came into view and my father pulled the Cutlass over and idled at the curb. "Now I want you two to study hard and not be stupes," he said.

"How can we study if we haven't had classes yet?" Ben asked.

"You will soon enough, wise guy."

I left the car that morning thinking how hard it was

for our father to praise us. He was quick to praise other kids but seldom had anything good to say about Ben or me. I thought about how his uncles had put on blackface and popped out of the bushes to scare him when he was a little boy. He'd told me about the beatings he'd received while being raised hanai in Kaimuki. Granny had run out of money and she was forced to rent her porch to a star boarder named Dad Hinkle. Dad slept outside under the overhang with a mosquito net draped over him; he hated "numbah one boy" because he was Granny's favorite and he used a manta ray's tail to whip my father at the slightest provocation. My father lost Dad's redwood board in heavy surf at Sunset Beach and Dad hung him by the ankles off a kiawe tree when Granny was at the store. He begged his uncles to cut him free but they only laughed and danced the hula around him.

*   *   *

At Punahou, our building was named Bishop Hall to honor a missionary who'd brought God to the Hawaiians. It was a stocky four-story built as wide as it was high on a hill overlooking a row of date palms. Bishop Hall was painted battleship gray and it had a roof that resembled a green umbrella. The grounds were landscaped with hala and coconut trees. Walls of lava rock fringed the walkways. Antherium bushes, ferns, ti plants, and crotons filled in the shady areas. Asian workmen were always busy clipping shrubs, raking, and watering.

Punahou existed because a missionary had discovered a stream bubbling beside the prop roots of a hala tree. The hala became symbolic of the school and its image appeared on the football helmets, the stationery, and the report cards. The stream that came from the tree pooled beside Thurston Chapel to form a pond. The pond was full of big green lily pads, frogs, and guppies. Alumni had elevated the pond to mythic proportions— weddings and luaus were held beside its waters.

While the nuns at Star of the Sea struck the tops of our hands with rulers and whacked our okoles with yardsticks, corporeal punishment was forbidden at Punahou. Boys tied window blind cords to chairs and hung the chairs out of fourth floor windows. Spray painting lockers and blowing up toilets were also in fashion. The smell of cigarettes permeated the bathrooms. On Mrs. Kalipi's birthday, someone put a present on her desk before Social Studies. Mrs. Kalipi always wore a muumuu and a shiny kukui nut lei to class. "How sweet," she said when she entered the room and saw the gift. She smiled reading the attached card. We watched her remove the wrapping from a bottle of Scope. The boys in back snickered. Mrs. Kalipi took out a Kleenex from her purse and dabbed her eyes. "To Mr. Anonymous," she said, "mahalo for your generosity."

*   *   *

The teachers were showered with gifts that first semester: Mr. Tenant got a jockstrap; Mrs. Finch received a copy of *Playboy Magazine*; Mr. Boone ended up with a Weight Watchers cookbook. Someone cut open the canvas roof on Mr. Krueger's Mercedes roadster, released the parking brake, and let it roll down the hill. The roadster jumped a curb and was totaled when it struck a date palm. Not to be outdone, the Mad Bomber flushed charges with underwater fuses in three toilets in the Boys' basement bathroom. The porcelain cracked and the water main blew. The police were notified but no one ever discovered the Mad Bomber's identity.

KILLAHAOLE DAY

Killahaole Day took place the last day of class on Oahu. You took the risk of being pummeled by a Hawaiian classmate if you were haole and went to school that day. Tom Wrigley had gotten his teeth shattered by a lead pipe. If you were hapa haole like me, your fate was determined by how white you looked. I worked hard on my tan the last month of school. Some haoles were dying their hair and eyebrows dark.

Being born and raised in the islands didn't make you Hawaiian. "Hawaiian" meant you were related to the Polynesians who'd discovered Hawaii. Asian, Puerto Rican, and Portuguese boys weren't targeted because Hawaiians considered them descendants of the laborers brought in to work the white man's plantations. Killahaole Day was a day of retribution. It was based on the fact that the sons of white missionaries had imprisoned Queen Lili'uokalani and declared Hawaii a republic for their own profit. To Hawaiians, names such as Dole, Thurston, and Bishop hung over Oahu like a curse. Buildings, streets, and companies that carried those names were reminders that the white man ruled. You couldn't blame Hawaiians for having pakalaki feelings. Frustration over losing the aina was intensified by the stereotype that natives were lazy and uneducated. A partner had voted against my father becoming an associate upon discovering he had Hawaiian blood.

The nuns at Star of the Sea ruled with iron fists but they retreated to the safety of their convent when the last bell of the school year sounded. My Hawaiian classmates didn't bug me because, besides looking local, I'd written and directed a play about pro wrestlers defeating a gang of vampire surfers. *Pipeline Bloodsuckers* had made me a celebrity. Ben wasn't as fortunate—he wasn't a playwright and his blond hair and green eyes made him stand out. To make matters worse, he'd earned a reputation as a con artist. Ben was a ringer when it came to the game of marbles. He challenged me every day after school and, when I got tired of losing, he'd pull out a second marble and play himself. On the marble fields of Star of the Sea, Ben disguised his skills in "for fun" games that he purposely lost. After bolstering the confidence of his mark, he'd pull out his rare aquamarine cat's eye and suggest a game of "kini keeps." This meant the marbles on the playing field were up for grabs and, if you lost, you couldn't exchange a valuable marble for a lesser one. Ben usually hit an opponent's marble by his third shot and it wasn't long before he'd won

Ricky Aikau's prized agate. Ricky was his classmate and he demanded a rematch. Ben refused. Then Ben threw a rock into a crowd on the first day of Lent—the rock bounced off Ricky's head. Ricky retaliated by organizing a gang that chased Ben into the foothills above the school.

In sixth grade, I'd witnessed the Killahaole Day fight between Ben and Ricky's gang. They'd trapped him on the gravel road behind the thrift shop. The shop was closed. At first it didn't seem serious—just a group of Catholic boys in white button-downs and khaki pants going through a ritual that would amount to nothing more than name calling and idle threats. Ricky pushed Ben. Ben pushed Ricky back. A boy named Freitas and his friend Mits began pelting Ben with gravel. The sun was below the roof of the convent and only a few cars were in the parking lot.

A Hawaiian kid we all called "Da Destroya" walked out from behind the thrift shop. His sleeves were rolled over his biceps and he was wielding a Louisville Slugger. His skin was the color of koa and he was Father Keelan's height. He'd been held back for punching a nun in the guts after she struck him with a yardstick. He kept a bench and weights in the bushes behind the shop and worked out during recess and lunch. I'd seen him belt three homers over the fence on All Saints' Day. Da Destroya had been one of my wrestlers in *Pipeline Bloodsuckers* and, in the final act, he lifted a vampire over his head. He had wanted to be a vampire but, since he was the only actor who could lift anyone, I made him a wrestler instead.

Da Destroya took a vicious cut with the bat at a bush

of red hibiscus—a flower flew like a missile toward the convent. Geckos scrambled up the thrift shop wall. He jammed the cap of the bat into Ben's belly and Ben dropped to his knees.

Ricky stood over my brother like a boxer who'd just knocked his opponent to the canvas. "Ya goin' catch dirty lickins," he said.

I looked across main field at the church. It was an A-frame with a steel cross embedded in its lava facade. We had all received First Holy Communion there and I wondered how violence could erupt so close to its doors. It was as if the green-winged devil I'd seen in my illustrated Bible was winning the battle for souls. I headed for the gravel road. Mits turned around and gave me the stink eye; he was a short, stocky Japanese boy who'd bragged about his yellow belt in karate. Ben had told him yellow was the perfect color for him because the Japanese were cowards for their sneak attack on Pearl Harbor.

Ben got off his knees and pressed his back to the thrift shop wall. His shirt and pants were stained with dirt and dots of blood freckled his arms where he'd been cut by the gravel. Freitas and Mits continued to pelt him.

I put my books down and stood in front of Ben while the gravel rained down. The stones stung and I put my hands up to protect my face.

"Outta da way!" Freitas said.

Ben hid his hands in his pockets. "Scram, Peanut."

"I'm not scramming."

"Time out!" Ricky said. He pulled a small wax bag

of cinnamon toothpicks from his shirt pocket and placed a toothpick in the corner of his mouth. Da Destroya rested the bat on his shoulder and snatched two toothpicks. Freitas and Mits dropped their gravel and pulled toothpicks from the bag.

I was almost certain Ricky would leave me alone because I was a grade below him. It was common knowledge that the Hawaiian boys in your class had exclusive rights on Killahaole Day because they could best judge how much punishment to inflict.

Ricky sucked his toothpick. "Yoa bruddah goin' die," he told me.

"Thou Shalt Not Kill Haoles," I said.

"Dat's no Commandment," said Freitas. He blocked one of his nostrils with a finger and blew out a blast of snot. He was a fat boy whose mother deep-fried dough for the Coffee & Malasada gatherings after Mass on Sundays.

I pointed at the church. "Let He Who Has Not Sinned Cast The First Stone."

"Shut yoa fuckin' mout'," Ricky snarled.

"Yeah," said Mits, "befoah I geev ya karate chop."

Da Destroya took the bat off his shoulder and rested the cap on the ground. He pulled the toothpicks out of his mouth. "Jesus say dat 'bout stones?"

"Yeah," I answered, "in the New Testament."

"Fuck ya haole Jesus," Ricky told me.

Da Destroya examined his toothpicks before putting them back in his mouth. He lifted the bat and whacked the bush. This time two flowers shattered and a mantis flew over the roof of the thrift shop. "My muddah pray Jesus," Da Destroya said. "She stay ova at Queen's."

"She sick?" I asked.

He leaned the bat against the thrift shop wall and headed for the steps. He climbed slowly. He spit out the toothpicks when he reached the top step. "She get cancah," he told me.

When Da Destroya lost his desire to clobber my brother, so did the rest of the gang. Mits and Freitas quit crowding in and Ricky paced over the gravel road. Ben scooted past the hibiscus bush and hurried for the cyclone fence. He zipped through the gate and jogged the sidewalk of Kalanianiole Highway. The white tails of his shirt flapped behind him like surrender flags.

Ricky turned to me. "Tell ya bruddah we get um first t'ing next yee-ah."

"No can," I said.

"Whacha mean 'no can?' "

"Ben's going to Punahou," I said, "and so am I."

"Fuckin' haole school," muttered Ricky. "I get um afta Church."

Freitas nodded. "Durin' Coffee & Malasada."

"Ben doesn't go to Church anymore," I said. "He's an atheist."

Ricky strolled over to the thrift shop, picked up the bat, and turned to me. "Den yoa goin' take his place."

"Yeah," Mits said, "geev um one good whippin'."

I tried running but Mits grabbed me, spun me around, and got me in a full nelson. It was a hold we'd all learned watching Honolulu All-Star Wrestling every Saturday. I kicked his shin. Mits punished me by squeezing harder. My arms dangled helplessly as he applied more and more pressure. It felt as though my head was being stretched away from my body.

Freitas stabbed my forearm with his toothpick.

"Owie!" I said.

Ricky approached with the bat. "Ya goin' say moah dan 'owie,' " he promised. He took a practice swing and the air rushed past the barrel.

"But I wrote that play," I pleaded, "about vampires."

"I no care," Ricky said and faked a swing to my head.

"I no care eitha," Freitas chimed in.

"Eh!" Da Destroya said from the top step.

Ricky turned around. "What?"

"Leave um alone."

"Who says?"

"Me."

Ricky took another practice swing and spit out his toothpick.

"Why?" Da Destroya asked. "Ya like beef, ya fuckin' kanaka?"

Ricky lowered the bat and glared at me. He nodded at Mits to let me go.

I hustled over and picked up Ben's books. His report card was lying in the dirt and I picked that up too. I stacked my books on top of Ben's and ran for the fence. I got halfway and looked back—Ricky and his gang were smoking on the steps of the thrift shop.

Da Destroya had left. He was moving through the field of dirt and crab grass where he'd hit his homers. His strides were long and determined.

He was heading for the church.

*   *   *

Killahaole Day was not a rite of passage at Punahou. The boys were mostly haole and Asian, and the Asians were more interested in getting good grades than seeking revenge for their forefathers' sufferings in the pineapple and cane fields. But for haoles in the public school system, every day was Killahaole Day. I learned that when I took the Punahou bus home. Ben didn't ride with me because he played after-school football. My bus was known as "Da Fuckin' Haole Bus" by locals. It was easy to identify because it was blue and more modern than the regular yellow buses; it had tinted windows that slid open sideways instead of up and down. The mayor had received a huge campaign contribution from a Punahou grad so he assigned our school one of the new buses he'd purchased in Texas with city money. The bus began its route on Palm Drive and headed for the haole enclaves along Kahala Avenue and Diamond Head Road before ending up in Waikiki. The only stipulation was that we stop for passengers since the city had paid for the bus.

The first time I took Da Fuckin' Haole Bus, I wondered why all the Kahala boys got off early in Waialae. Felix, the Filipino driver, drove by a dirt baseball diamond. Quonset huts were covered with graffiti and the plumeria trees had been stripped of their flowers. Kids congregated at a bus stop next to a bench with missing slats.

A Japanese boy sat across the aisle from me. Pens and mechanical pencils were clipped to his shirt pocket and his books were stuffed into a JAL tote bag that rested beside him on the bench seat.

"What school's this?" I asked him.

He frowned at me and looked through his window. "Kaimuki Elementary."

"Do the boys bug you?"

"The Portagees call me 'rice ball.' "

"You should call them 'greasy malasadas.' "

"And get beat up? No, thanks."

"What's your name?" I asked.

"Sheldon."

Outside, boys were taking turns pushing one other off the curb. Someone kicked a bottle into the street and it shattered. The bus squealed to a stop and a glob of spit hit the windshield. "Ai-ya," Felix said and turned on the wipers. He pulled a lever and the hydraulic door opened. The big boys crowded on. They wore wide leather watchbands and had cigarettes tucked behind their ears. Only a few carried books. Three boys had words carved in their forearms: two were Hawaiian and the third was Portuguese. One of the Hawaiian boys was wiry and the other was husky. The Portuguese boy had dirty blond hair and a face full of pimples—he held a bottle wrapped in a paper bag.

The wiry boy reached my seat first. I saw "Kimo" in the oozy, pus-filled scabs on his forearm.

"Wheah ya go school, punk?" Kimo asked me.

The cover of the spiral notebook on my lap read: "Punahou School, Established 1841," under a gold hala tree. The husky boy peered down over Kimo's shoulder. I knew I was in big trouble, but that I'd be in bigger trouble if I lied. "Punahou," I said.

"Fuckin' haole," the husky boy muttered. "T'ink yoa moah betta dan us?"

"No."

"Ya ain't nut'in', punk," Kimo said as two Japanese girls squeezed by. Kimo pulled a black marker out of his pocket and wrote KIMO-n-CHARLENE FOREVAHS on the steel frame of the bus. Sheldon took his tote bag off the seat and held it on his lap.

The Portuguese boy wedged his way between Kimo and the husky boy. He looked like an eighth grader. "Fuckin' haole," he said. He wore a red T-shirt and pineapple pants. Sweat rings darkened the fabric under his pits. His pants had scenes of grass shack villages, double-hulled canoes, and warriors with spears. His nostrils flared with every breath. The scabby letters on his arm spelled: "Sweetbread." He had dirt under his fingernails and he smelled like old cheese. Sweetbread opened his paper bag, pulled out a quart bottle of Colt 45, and unscrewed the cap.

Kimo grabbed the bottle, took a pull, and gargled before swallowing.

A Chinese girl in a micromini walked up to Kimo. Her legs were long and lean. "Gimmee one sip," she said.

"Make it, Joy. Go wait wit' Charlene."

Joy headed for the big bench seat in back.

"Whacha lookin' at, haole boy?" Sweetbread asked me.

"Nothing."

"Nut'in', my okole." He pulled the bottle away from Kimo and guzzled the Colt 45. His Adam's apple bobbed up and down.

"You're haole too," I said.

Sweetbread spewed out a stream of malt liquor that hit Sheldon. Kimo laughed. Sheldon pulled a handkerchief out of his shirt pocket and dried off his face and tote bag.

"Whacha say?" Sweetbread asked me.

"Your hair's blond, isn't it?"

Kimo and the husky boy elbowed one other as the bus continued to fill with passengers.

"Only da kine hairdressa knows foa shu-ah," Kimo teased.

Two rail-thin Filipinas walked by in bellbottoms. One snapped gum in her mouth and the other lit up a Kool. Smoke drifted through the bus like fog.

Sweetbread crumpled his paper bag into a ball and bounced it off my head. I ignored him and he punched my shoulder. It hurt but it was no harder than one of Ben's punches. "Ya like t'row?" he asked, his invitation to a fistfight.

"You're bigger than me," I said.

"So?"

"So, so, suck yoa toe," Kimo told Sweetbread.

The hydraulic door closed and the bus lurched forward. Sweetbread lost his balance and he grabbed my hair to steady himself. He coughed up phlegm and spit on the empty seat in front of mine. "Sit on my hanabuttah."

"You sit on it," I said.

"Huh?"

"What are you," I answered, "deaf?"

Sweetbread capped his bottle, handed it to Kimo, and dug the fingernails of both hands into the back of my neck. My neck began to sting.

"Choke um," Kimo said.

"Kill um," the husky boy said.

"I like one sip!" a girl begged.

"Shuddup, Charlene," Sweetbread said and kept squeezing. I hunched my shoulders to give him less neck to squeeze.

"I get da kine clove cigarette," Charlene said and lured Kimo and the husky boy back.

Sweetbread continued squeezing. My windpipe constricted and I started to gag.

"I no moah da kine unduh-weah," Joy confessed.

Sweetbread released his grip. "Fuckin' lucky," he said, "ya fuckin' haole." He headed to the back of the bus.

*   *   *

I never got off early that first week of riding Da Fuckin' Haole Bus. I was the only Punahou student left by the time the bus reached Kaimuki Elementary. Even Sheldon was exiting in Waialae. I was rewarded by being punched twice in the belly by Kimo and getting spit on by

Sweetbread. I saw Felix watching through his side view mirror when Sweetbread dropped a lit butt into the hood of my windbreaker. I felt the heat climbing up my neck as the butt smoldered

"Burn, haole, burn," Sweetbread said.

"Stinkin' fuckin' haole," said Kimo.

Joy and Charlene giggled and held their noses.

*   *   *

I tied a pillow to a wooden support post on the lanai. I was punching it when my father got home from work. His gray coat was slung over one shoulder and he frowned through the glass doors. He put his briefcase and coat on a chair and came outside. Yardley Brilliantine gave his hair a flat, shiny quality and his five o'clock shadow made him look mean.

"Hi, Daddy," I said.

"What the hell's this malarkey?"

"I'm learning how to box."

"You'd better not damage that post."

"I won't," I said hitting the pillow with my bare knuckles. I hit harder now that my father was watching and my knuckles ached.

"You punch like a li'l girl," my father said.

I lowered my hands.

My father removed his tie. He rolled his sleeves over his forearms, straightened his back, and took a boxer's stance. He reminded me of a fencer the way he turned to his side and threw out his left as if lunging with a sword. He showed me how to hold my hands, how to step into a punch, and how to avoid getting hit. He danced on the balls of his feet in his oxblood shoes and hit the pillow with one-two combinations. His Uncle Sharkey had taught him the basics when a bully at Saint Louis threatened to beef him; the day after his first lesson, he beat the bully up.

"Is someone bothering you at Punahou?" my father asked.

"No," I answered, "just some kids on the bus."

"Nip it in the bud," he advised. "Once you let a bully push you around, he'll keep on pushing 'til you do something about it."

"I will."

"Will what?"

"Do something."

He tapped his belly with an open palm. "Hit me in the guts," he said.

"I don't wanna hurt you."

"You won't. Go on. Hard as you want."

I made a fist with my left hand and punched him lightly above the belly button.

"Come on. A wahine could hit harder."

I swung again and hit near his belly button. He had flab around his middle but I felt the muscle underneath.

"Is that the best you've got, sissy boy?" he asked. "You'll never beat up a bully punching like that. Try again."

I really wound up this time and put my weight behind the blow. My fist made a popping sound when it struck his solar plexus.

My father let out a gasp. "See that?" he asked. "I'm

made of iron."

"You're ol' iron gut," I joked.

"What are you made of, Jeffrey?"

"Something really really strong."

"Like what?"

"Steel," I replied. "I'm made of steel."

                    *   *   *

I wasn't made of steel. Even though my boxing skills improved, I never worked up the courage to challenge Sweetbread. I wished Ben was there so we could fight as a team. He told me I was a fool for taking kukae. The day after Sweetbread held the cold blade of his butterfly knife against my throat, I passed on Da Fuckin' Haole Bus and took an old yellow bus home. I don't know why I didn't just get off in Waialae. I guess I didn't want to give them the satisfaction of forcing me to walk the extra mile home even though the yellow bus took an extra hour because I had to transfer lines in Moiliili. My bad feelings were tempered by remembering the day Da Destroya had showed me mercy. I kept seeing him walking alone across main field at Star of the Sea and I wondered how he was doing and if his mother was still alive.

DEBBIE MILLS

I gained a measure of popularity at Punahou after Reverend Wigton, my longhaired teacher for Bible Studies, was arrested in Thurston Chapel for torching the ROTC Armory at UH. It was the same armory my father had guarded the day Pearl Harbor was bombed. Reverend Wigton stood in the pulpit reciting New Testament passages to our class when HPD arrived with reporters from *Channel 2 Eyewitness News*.

"Five-O!" my classmate Brian Ching called out.

Reverend Wigton closed the Bible. He stepped down from the pulpit and was cuffed beside the altar. But before our teacher was led away, we joined hands and formed a ring around him.

"We shall overcome," a girl began to sing.

We all sang along. Our singing grew stronger and stronger. I had never heard such passion in voices. The news cameras were rolling. Eventually, the police got sick of our protest and broke through the ring. I appeared in the background on the news that night.

"That Wigton's a god damn hippie," my father said as he watched.

"He's just sick of people dying in Vietnam," I argued.

"I hope they give that arsonist thirty years."

"You sing well, Jeffrey," my mother commented.

My father frowned. "He sounded like a sissy."

At school I was considered one of the "Punahou Twenty," those brave students who'd refused to turn their antiwar leader over to the cops. *Ka Punahou*, the school newspaper, interviewed me. My comment about seeking peace on earth made the front page, along with a photo of us with our hands linked around Wigton. A high school girl wrote a play about the arrest and performances were held at Thurston Chapel on weekends. Brian Ching landed a supporting role and once again said, "Five-O!" as boys in police uniforms charged the altar. Every performance was sold out.

*   *   *

After my celebrity status wore off and I was reduced to one of the minions, identical twins everyone called "the Twinkies" approached me out by the lockers on the fourth floor. They had red hair, blue eyes, and were as tall as the guys in high school. They smelled like smoke and their fingernails were bloody from chewing.

"We're watching you," the first Twinkie said.

I could see a pack of Marlboros through the fabric of the second Twinkie's shirt pocket.

The first Twinkie slugged me in the left shoulder. "You're old news."

"How old?" I teased.

"Way old," said the second Twinkie and he punched me in the right shoulder.

They walked off and swung open the door to the Boys' bathroom. A desk was out in the hallway and I shoved it against the bathroom door before heading down the stairs. By the time I'd reached the ground floor, I heard the Twinkies shouting and banging for help.

*   *   *

Ben asked me which girls I liked at Punahou.

"You go first, Juicy," I said, suspicious of his intentions.

"Suzie Garza."

"Who's she?"

He said Suzie was a Brazilian girl in the eighth grade and I asked him how much he liked her and he said a little. He said they made out before her Science class after he took off his headgear.

"Now who do you dig?" Ben asked me.

"Debbie Mills."

"She's in my History class," Ben replied, "and I'm going to tell her."

"You'd better not!"

"I will unless you fork over a buck."

I paid the bribe because I didn't want Debbie knowing until I told her myself.

*   *   *

Lucy Seville, a coquettish brunette with a shag hairdo, had the locker above mine in the hallway. Every morning we walked from our lockers down to Study Hall. She told me her father was Dr. Seville, the junior high principal. We sat at neighboring desks and, one morning, Lucy sprang up and performed dance steps she'd learned at Kini's Dance Studio in Kailua. Miss Molly, our wizened no-nonsense supervisor, watched Lucy gyrate without reprimanding her.

"What's that dance?" I asked Lucy as she shimmied in her white go-go boots and suede skirt.

"The Monkey," she answered. "Isn't it just the coolest?"

"You remind me of Judy on *Laugh In*."

She stopped dancing and grabbed my hand. "You really think so?"

"You could be her kid sister."

Lucy squeezed my hand. "Righteous!"

I liked Lucy. She had dimples when she smiled and always wore mod clothes. I watched her doodle on her desktop. Boys avoided her because she was the principal's daughter. I'm sure Lucy would have run with the cool crowd had she not been related to Dr. Seville. I wondered if her father understood how much he was damaging his daughter's social life just by sitting in his office on the first floor.

*   *   *

If love at first sight was possible, Debbie Mills was that possibility for me. We both had Homeroom with Mrs.

Finch, a birdlike woman who taught geography. Homeroom met every morning for half-an-hour before first period. I sat right behind Debbie and I was next to a window so I had a great view of her profile. I'd stare at her reflection on cloudy mornings when the window was a mirror. Debbie had short blonde hair that reminded me of a halo. I loved the freckles on her nose and how her arms were always tan. I'd been used to Star of the Sea girls marching single file in white blouses and blue plaid skirts; hemlines fell below the knees and baggy blouses hid arms and shoulders. Sometimes I'd catch myself gazing longingly at a calf or an ankle and feel a tinge of guilt as Thou Shalt Not Covet Thy Neighbor's Wife entered my mind. Then I realized these girls weren't married and it was okay to look.

Debbie was different than the Star of the Sea girls. A big part of that difference was that Punahou required no uniform. Debbie's miniskirts challenged Punahou's rule that hemlines could be no higher than three inches above the knee. Mrs. Finch used a green ruler to measure the space between Debbie's knee and her hemline and, when she held the ruler against Debbie's thigh, my insides cried out. Debbie reminded me of Michelangelo's angels in the Sistine Chapel—lithe and spiritual yet full of passion. She deserved nothing less than absolute worship.

*   *   *

Ben sat in the front seat and I sat in back when our father drove us to school in his Cutlass. The car was a two-door with an AM radio and dual speakers. We listened to

KGMB's J. Akuhead Pupule, a local who'd made his mark with biting commentary about Honolulu's political landscape. Akuhead interspersed his diatribes with songs ranging from Kui Lee's "I'll Remember You" to "Love Child" by The Supremes. From the back seat I studied the scar on my father's right hand, the hand that held the wheel. The scar was in the web of flesh between his thumb and index finger. He'd been bodysurfing off Cape Halawa on Moloka'i when an ulua line with a steel leader hooked his hand and he struggled underwater to free himself, coming up for air in five-foot swells. He couldn't walk the line in because it was connected to seven other ulua lines that stretched across a quarter-mile of ocean bottom. He thought about sharks. They would come from the deep blue when they smelled blood and he figured the first shark would be a hammerhead since he'd killed one in Pailolo Channel. He was tempted to yank the hook sideways and rip the flesh. Instead, he patiently worked the hook back and forth and bit the skin away where the barb had set. He tugged the leader and the hook came free.

It was hard imagining my father being young. It was as if came out of the womb wearing glasses, with all the joy and wonder squeezed out of him. We drove past the manicured lawns of Kaimuki and my father switched off the radio. The scent of his Brilliantine made me nauseous. He reached under his seat and pulled out a cardboard box. We took the ramp leading to the H-1 Freeway and he lifted the cover off the box and pulled out a card. "I want definitions for these words," my father said merging into freeway traffic.

"What's this," Ben said, "*Jeopardy*?"

"Okay, Jeffrey," my father said, "your word is 'detrimental.' "

"Can you use it in a sentence?"

"Cigarettes are detrimental to your health."

"Bad," I answered.

"Incorrect," my father said. "It means harmful."

"Isn't bad close enough?"

"No." He grabbed another card. "Okay, Ben," he said, "iconoclastic."

"Constipated," Ben blurted.

My father quizzed us every morning on our way to school. If you got a word wrong, he'd go on to the next card to find out just how dumb you were. "God damn stupe," he'd say, "we just had that one last week." Ben had so much trouble that I started slipping him answers scrawled on notebook paper. The torture continued until my father pulled off the H-1 onto Wilder Avenue.

"If you boys don't start remembering," he said, "you'll never get ahead." He wanted us to be lawyers. He discouraged rival professions by focusing on humbling images: pilots had mindless jobs since they flew the same routes day in and day out; architects spent their time hunched over drafting tables; dentists stood on their feet all day smelling halitosis; doctors breathed the germs of sick people; surgeons got their hands soaked with blood. He told us if we continued to get our vocabulary words wrong we'd end up as clerks.

"What do clerks do?" I asked him.

"File papers and take orders."

Ben squirmed in the front seat. "How much do they make?"

"Clerks don't have a pot to pee in."

"Why do they even work?" I asked.

"To feed their god damn families."

"I wanna be a scientist," I said, "like Tom Swift."

"I suppose you get straight As in science and math?"

"No."

"You'll never be a scientist."

"I wanna be a stuntman," Ben said, "in Hollywood."

My father pulled his Cutlass over in front of the school and frowned at Ben. "Start saving for your funeral."

THE PUNAHOU CARNIVAL

By the spring semester, junior high boys and girls were beginning to pair up. The catalyst for these love matches was the Punahou Carnival, the biggest and best on Oahu because of its rides, food and game booths, and a white elephant tent stocked with alumni donations ranging from Tiki lamps to Vegematics to 14 carat gold ku'uipo bracelets. High school students were responsible for manning the booths with the help of alumni volunteers.

Bishop Hall buzzed with gossip about who was taking whom to the carnival. Suzie Garza turned Ben down because a sophomore from Roosevelt High had asked her to go steady. Rumors spread that some of our seventh grade girls were smoking pakalolo, dropping acid, and going all the way with older guys. I hadn't heard any rumors about Debbie but I'd seen the way boys checked her out. I didn't ask her to the carnival because I was scared she'd turn me down. Debbie reminded me of Helen of Troy and remained in a sacred place in my soul because, whenever I felt bad about myself, fantasizing about being with her helped me escape into a bright new world.

On Thursday, the day before the carnival, I saw Lucy out by the lockers. She looked foxy in her tie-dye blouse and button-down jeans. Her light brown hair was no longer in the shag style she wore at the start of the school year— now it hung just above her shoulders.

Lucy spun the dial on her combination lock. "Wanna go to the carnival, Jeff?"

The way she asked such a serious question so nonchalantly put me at ease. "Okay," I answered.

"You know we go half-day tomorrow, right?"

"We do?"

"Sure," Lucy replied digging through clothes and books in her locker. "Everyone in junior high is free by noon and that's when the carnival officially starts. But all the other kids from all the other schools have to stay in school 'til three. We get first dibs on all the rides and games and malasadas. I'll meet you here tomorrow and we can go down and have some peachy keen fun."

"Peachy keen," I said.

"You don't seem very stoked, Jeff."

"I'm just worried about my algebra test."

Lucy shut her locker. "I know the best cure for worry."

"What's that, Lucy?"

"I'll show you tomorrow," she giggled and dashed down the hall.

*   *   *

I met Lucy at the lockers the next day at noon and we walked out of Bishop Hall and down the hill. She wore a purple miniskirt, white go-go boots, a paisley headband, and a strand of love beads. She smelled like pikake blossoms. She had on pink lipstick, matching fingernail polish, and carried a leather handbag with fringes. I wore faded blue jeans that were hand-me-downs from Ben, a green Ski Hawaii T-shirt, and flip-flops. I was challenging Punahou's rules for personal grooming by growing my hair out over my ears. Brian Ching had said longer hair made me look local.

"Cool duds, Lucy," I said.

"Ditto, Jeff."

The carnival took up Palm Drive and most of lower field. The white elephant tent was huge—it loomed over the outdoor basketball courts and resembled the big top at a circus with its red and white stripes. The field where we played soccer and baseball was covered with rides and Palm Drive swarmed with students, teachers, and alumni. A layer of straw on the asphalt gave the carnival a circus feel. Ben and his friend Pierre Fong stood near the basketball toss holding Cokes and gobbling down meat sticks. "Basketball's for geeks," Ben said. My teachers Mr. Elders and Mrs. Finch made a beeline for the white elephant tent. Giant monkeypod trees and date palms shaded the booths. Some of the juniors were putting last minute brush strokes on their plywood fronts and the smell of wet paint mingled with the aroma of frying malasadas. A sound system had been set up and a boy kept repeating, "Testing, testing, one, two, three, four," over the speakers.

We headed to the Scrip Booth and I exchanged the five dollars my father had given me for fifty scrip. Lucy bought ten dollars worth but she said she couldn't spend it all on herself because she had to use some of it to buy her father a birthday present at the white elephant.

The carnival's theme was "Feelin' Groovy" and the high school students had named their booths "Outta Site Meat Sticks," "Corn on the Righteous Cob," and "Bitchin Saimin." The games featured "Hippie Dippy Darts" and "Janis Joplin Ring Toss." You could kiss runner-ups from the Miss Hawaii pageant at a booth called "Sock It To Me, Baby." Lucy and I walked along Palm Drive to Flip Your Wig Malasadas. An Asian lady fished golden brown malasadas from a bubbling vat of oil and tossed them in a bin of sugar. She used a pair of metal tongs to move the hot malasadas around in the sugar until they sparkled.

"How many?" asked the lady.

"Two," I said.

"What?" she asked me. "No moah appetite?"

"I have to save scrip for the games and rides."

The lady nodded and put our malasadas in a bag and Lucy and I ate as we strolled past the booths. The malasadas were still hot so we licked the sugar off the sides before nibbling on the fried dough. It was like a doughnut, only better because the dough was thick and super sweet. We got within range of the midway. Kids screamed on the Twister ride and I saw the Ferris Wheel rotating through the branches of a plumeria tree. We talked about school as we finished our malasadas. Lucy told me it wasn't easy being the principal's daughter.

"Everyone thinks I'm a narc," she said.

"Aren't you?" I joked.

"Jeffrey Gill," she said, "you are such a brat."

"Wanna go on a ride?"

"The Tilt-A-Whirl!"

"What's that?"

"Only the most righteous ride on earth," she said and grabbed my hand.

We jogged past the cotton candy concession and reached the midway. The grass on lower field was already turning yellow from people trampling on it. The metal arms of the rides stretched like tentacles over the field. Lucy led me to a ride where red cars with hulls shaped like soupspoons rolled over a circular track of hills and valleys. Each car had the ability to pivot and that allowed it to spin if the riders shifted their weight in the same direction. A carny with greasy jeans and silver teeth manipulated the speed of the cars with a lever and chuckled when the girls on his ride screamed.

Lucy opened her handbag. "This is my treat," she said and traded ten scrip for two tickets at the Tilt-A-Whirl ticket booth. The ride stopped and Lucy chose a car perched on the high part of the track. We climbed in and the carny dropped down a metal safety bar that locked us in.

"Hand on da bah," the carny said.

I put my hands on the bar and so did Lucy. We

waited for the cars to fill with riders and soon the Tilt-A-Whirl's engine sputtered and eased to a steady tack-tack-tack. Our car lurched forward and we jerked down the track.

"Lean left!" Lucy ordered pressing her shoulder against my chest.

I hugged the car's side and it shifted on its pivot. We started to turn and I held on tight to the safety bar.

"We're tilting!" Lucy said. She took her hands off the safety bar and held them high in the air as if we were riding a roller coaster.

Our car rolled over the hill-and-valley track doing spins and half-turns. We took turns jamming our shoulders into one another to get our car to tilt on its pivot. Lucy's face turned red and her love beads swayed back and forth and clanked against the metal interior. I enjoyed the unpredictability of the ride, the way each dip in the track could change the movement of our car. And I didn't mind rubbing up against Lucy on the leans left and right. Her body felt good and I liked how she grabbed my forearm during our tilts. The ride ended in less than five minutes.

"Wanna go again?" Lucy asked.

"Let's play some games first," I suggested as the carny lifted the safety bar to set us free.

We ran over to the game booths. A clown walked by with a bouquet of helium balloons tethered to his wrist. Lucy tried Janis Joplin Ring Toss but managed to drop only one ring in four tries around a square frame. I played Hippie Dippy Darts and won Lucy a pink plush bunny by

breaking four balloons with five throws. I'd become fairly
good at darts because Ben had a dartboard in his room and,
when we got tired of tossing at the board, we'd throw darts
at each other; one of my darts hit Ben in the neck and I ran
to my room and locked the door to escape retribution.

Lucy buried her nose in the bunny's fur and came
up for air. "Wanna know what cures worry?" she asked.

"Sure."

"Close your eyes."

I shut my eyes halfway.

"Come on, Jeff, tight. Tight as a drum."

I closed them tight. I felt Lucy's breath on my cheek
and her lips against mine.

"There," she said, "how was that?"

I opened my eyes. "It was okay," I said, "but it hasn't
cured my worry."

"No?"

"Not yet."

She laughed. "What should I do about it?"

"Try again."

Lucy and I sat down under a hala tree. She kissed
me. Her lips were warm and moist. I kissed her back. She
nibbled on my ear lobe and we practiced kissing. Our teeth
bumped, we banged foreheads, and once she bit my tongue.
It wasn't long before I wore all the lipstick off Lucy's lips
and she had to reapply it. It was the first time I'd made out
and I liked the aroma of her pikake perfume and the way
she tasted like a malasada. We kissed until the shadows
from the booths and rides covered most of lower field and

children from the other schools began arriving. I spotted
Debbie out of the corner of my eye—she glided over to
Bitchin Saimin and stood in line. She was with an Asian
girl and I didn't want them to see me with Lucy. I stood up
and Lucy followed me over to Old School Hall on the high
school side of campus. It was quiet there and the carnival
seemed far away.

Lucy clutched the pink bunny with both hands and
held it against her belly. "Wanna go steady, Jeffy?" she
asked.

I studied the coral wall of the building. "Do I have
to buy you a ring or something?"

"No. Not if you don't want to."

I thought about Debbie. Even though I liked Lucy,
my heart was with another girl. I didn't want to hurt Lucy's
feelings but I had to be true to myself. It would be cheating
if I went steady with Lucy when I was thinking about
Debbie. "Can't we just be friends for now?" I asked.

Lucy looked away. "Okay, Jeff," she said, "that's
cool."

I had to leave Lucy to meet my father in front of the
Chink Store on his way home from work. On the drive
back to Kahala, I was proud of myself for getting way past
first base. It was hard not giving Lucy what she wanted
but leading her on could hurt her even more. I realized
Debbie was back at the carnival enjoying the food, games,
and rides. She would probably go on the Tilt-A-Whirl and
learn how to lean into the turns and tilt with someone else.
The girl of my dreams was busy making memories without

me. By the time my father pulled into the driveway, I was overwhelmed with guilt for leaving Lucy all alone outside Old School Hall.

Everything cool about the day had vanished.

WOODSHOP

The first day of eighth grade was the worst day of my life. Debbie Mills was in the courtyard outside Bishop Hall holding hands with Wayne Braswell. Ben told me Wayne had treated Debbie to a summer of matinees, rides on his father's catamaran, and cheeseburger lunches at the Outrigger Canoe Club. The girl I loved was going steady with the guy I couldn't stand. I'd hated Wayne ever since seventh grade. He was a big kid with dirty blond hair who thought he could get away with anything because his father was the city prosecutor. He'd thrown pineapple wedges at me during lunch and pushed me in the lily pond one morning after chapel. Seeing Wayne with Debbie made me sick. She wasn't in my new Homeroom and, except for Study Hall, she wasn't in any of my classes. I would see her in the hallway between classes and at Dole Cafeteria, where she'd be sitting with Wayne on the Pearl Harbor side. She seemed older somehow, as if by going steady she'd become more experienced and worldly. Once Debbie and I reached for the last butterscotch pudding and Wayne stretched his long arm over us and grabbed it. "Hey, Squirt," he said, "that's got my name on it."

They walked away and two ninth grade boys ogled Debbie.

"Choice babe," the first one said.

"Honey in the beehive," said the second.

*   *   *

Ben entered eighth grade more confident because he'd gotten his braces and headgear off after our summer on Moloka'i. He'd even talked our father into buying him contact lenses. My mother drove Ben to Kahala Mall and he returned with paisley shirts, corduroy pants, and Levi's bellbottoms. She'd asked me to go too but I couldn't stand shopping and was happy enough wearing hand-me-downs. Ben modeled the clothes for us and he looked like one of The Doors.

"Now, Ben," my father said, "I still want you wearing those black corrective shoes for your pigeon-toes."

Ben saluted. "Aye, aye, Captain."

My mother handed my father the bill.

"Cheesus," he said.

Ben wore his black shoes out of the house every morning. But he kept a pair of flip-flops in his locker that he put on as soon as he got to school. He also kept a can of Right Guard deodorant in the locker. He sprayed his pits before Homeroom because he'd overheard Cecily Hess say the scent of Right Guard drove her pupule with desire.

*   *   *

Study Halls were staggered throughout the day to give every student an hour with Miss Molly. Lucy wasn't in my Study Hall anymore but Debbie was. I knew this was my chance to get to know her but we rarely made eye contact—her desk was in the front row and mine was ten rows behind.

I shared back-to-back classes with Ben in the morning: Study Hall and Woodshop. I spent my Study Hall time doodling in my spiral notebook, scribbling graffiti on the wooden desk with my pencil, and daydreaming about Debbie. Students were carving initials and dirty words in the wood with paper clips and ballpoint pens. The bell rang ending Study Hall and I told Ben I'd seen a silver half-dollar in the lily pond.

"Sure it was a half-dollar?" he asked.

"Pretty sure."

"Wanna cut Woodshop?"

"Yeah," I said, "that class is a royal drag."

We headed over to the lily pond and I thought about all the boys sawing and shaping blocks of wood and how I wouldn't miss the smell of sawdust or the high-pitched moans from the lathes. The first assignment had been to make a wooden puzzle but I got the angles all wrong and Mr. Woodburn gave me a D-plus after he tried to make the pieces fit. Ben didn't do much better because he was more interested in working with metal than wood. I'd never been very good with my hands and the idea of making something conform to predetermined measurements was pure agony.

Ben and I strolled the banks of the lily pond. Dragonflies zipped over the surface and frogs croaked inside a clump of reeds. A white egret landed on the opposite side of the pond and scuttled into the water on long skinny legs.

I pointed to a glimmer between two lily pads. "There," I said.

Ben squinted. "That's only a quarter."

"Looks like a half-dollar to me."

"Water magnifies things," Ben said. He took off his flip-flops, rolled his cuffs over his knees, and waded out. A catfish resting on the bottom swam off.

"Hold on one minute!" a man said.

Mr. Tenant, a history teacher, had spotted us from across the field and now he was jogging over. He drove an MG to school and thought all the junior high girls were in love with him because he'd found a love note with juvenile sentiments under his windshield wiper. His hair was bright yellow and he always wore silk shirts and tight fitting pants, as if he had a second career as a model.

"What's that you're doing?" Tenant asked Ben.

"Cooling my toes."

"Why aren't you two in class?"

"Recess," I answered.

"Recess, eh?"

Ben climbed out of the pond, rolled down his cuffs, and stepped into his flip-flops. Tenant asked for our names and escorted us over to Bishop Hall where he had us wait on a long bench outside the principal's office. A redheaded woman sat at a tiny desk with a "Miss Patton" nameplate, a metal mesh basket for outgoing mail, and a silver intercom. Behind her was a door with "Dr. Seville" stenciled in black on the wood.

Tenant knocked on the door.

"Enter," came a gruff voice.

Tenant opened the door and, before it closed, I saw a silver-haired man sitting behind a desk. I heard muffled voices in the office as Miss Patton licked envelopes.

Tenant was out the door. "Won't be long now," he said sauntering down the hallway.

Ben gave him the finger. "What a mahu," he said.

Miss Patton looked over at us.

"Bring me the files for Benjamin and Jeffrey Gill," Seville said over the intercom.

Miss Patton popped up and slid open the middle drawer of a metal file cabinet. She flipped through a stack of manila folders.

"What's our story?" Ben asked me.

"I'll think of something."

Miss Patton glanced over at us and returned her attention to the folders. She found what she wanted, hustled over to the office, and opened the door. She walked in and closed the door immediately.

"Whacha think they're doing?" I asked.

"Monkeying," Ben replied.

Miss Patton was out in less than a minute. She returned to her chair and started clicking her pen.

"Send them in," Seville said.

"Okay, young men," Miss Patton said, "Dr. Seville will see you now."

Ben and I walked over to the door. I turned the knob and swung it open. Dr. Seville sat behind a massive desk wearing a brown suit and a blue tie. His office smelled like pipe tobacco.

"Hello, boys," Seville began.

"Hi, Dr. Seville," we said.

"Close that door and grab a seat."

Ben shut it. Two chairs were across from Seville and we sat down.

Seville's hair was combed back and it had an aluminum-like sheen. He had a big belly and broad shoulders. His hands reminded me of baseball mitts. He resembled LBJ because his face could shift from mean to kind and back to mean again in the blink of an eye. Piles of paper and manila folders covered his desk. A pair of tiny windows behind him overlooked Palm Drive and a jar of butterscotch candies was perched in a sill. On the wall was a framed photo of him with Mrs. Seville and Lucy in an outrigger canoe. It looked as if they'd just come from Church. The canoe was marooned on a strip of grass in front of the Hale Kuelani and Seville was seated at the stern holding a paddle. I was tempted to say I'd gone to the carnival with his daughter but figured that might make things worse.

Seville plucked two manila folders off a pile and opened them up. "So," he began, "I see I am graced by the presence of the Gill brothers today."

Ben and I nodded.

"Which one's Jeffrey and who's Ben?"

"I'm Jeff," I said.

Ben raised his hand. "Ben."

"Do you know why you're both here?"

Ben didn't respond so I decided to do the talking. "We were looking for turtles in the lily pond," I said.

"Young man, your parents don't pay tuition so you can look for turtles. It says in your Schedule of Classes you should both be at Woodshop with Mr. Woodburn."

"Mr. Woodburn said if we get ahead on projects we can take the day off," I pointed out.

"Oh, he did, did he?"

"Yes."

Seville clasped his hands behind his head and leaned back in his chair. "Was this your understanding too, Ben?"

"Yes, Dr. Seville."

Seville nodded. He picked up the phone and dialed. "Hello, Edward," Seville said, "this is Bob. I have two of your students in my office, the Gill brothers, and they tell me it's your policy to let achievers have the day off if they're ahead on their projects. Is this true? Oh, it is. I see. Are the Gills far ahead in your class? Well, isn't that interesting. Yes, that's good to know. Thank you, Edward. Right, see you at lunch." Seville hung up. He stared across the table at Ben until Ben looked away. Seville stared at me.

"How's good ol' Mr. Woodburn?" I asked.

Seville cleared his throat. "Good ol' Mr. Woodburn says that not only are you and your brother not ahead in his class, you're both three projects behind. If anyone shouldn't be missing Woodshop it's the two of you. You're both suspended for the remainder of the week."

"Does that mean we're expelled?" Ben asked.

"Not necessarily. However, suspension can lead to expulsion if you don't shape up."

"But Woodshop's for boys who wanna become carpenters," I argued. "Please give us a second chance, Dr. Seville. Kids are smoking and blowing up toilets and hanging chairs out of windows and you do nothing to them. It's just not fair."

Dr. Seville drummed his fingers on the table. "You did something worse than cutting class, young man."

"What?"

"You lied to me."

"I didn't say we were ahead," I replied, "I simply said it was Mr. Woodburn's policy."

"Don't know when to quit, do you, son? Have your father phone me first thing in the morning."

*   *   *

I was sitting on the living room couch between my mother and Ben when my father pulled into the driveway and parked. We'd kept the front door open so it would be one less obstacle after a hard day at work. Sometimes things went easier if you prepared for his arrival, such as having the *Honolulu Star-Bulletin* waiting for him on the dining room table and making sure the ice cube bucket was full of fresh cubes. My father shut his car door and his shoes clumped over the driveway. The front door slammed and he entered the living room.

"Who's keeping this front door wide open?" he demanded.

"Hello, Dear," my mother began, "did you have a nice day at the office?"

My father looked around the room suspiciously. The TV wasn't playing and Ben lowered his eyes.

"What's wrong?" my father asked.

"The boys had a little trouble today."

"Oh? And what kind of little trouble was that?"

"Dr. Seville wants you to phone him first thing in the morning. He suspended Ben and Jeffrey."

"Cheesus Holy Mother of Christ. What the hell happened?"

I told my version and Ben told his.

The more we pleaded our case the redder our father's face got. He took off his glasses and chewed on the stems. "Why the hell did you cut class if the first place?"

"We hate Woodshop," I said.

"You call that an excuse? I don't blame Dr. Seville for suspending you. You're both grounded."

"For how long?" Ben asked.

"For a million god damn years."

ABANDON SHIP

English was my favorite class in eighth grade because Mr. Krueger, a slight man with curly black hair, let us write stories. I wrote one about a talking parrot named Pygmalion that assumes more and more of his owner's identity until he phones in orders for bird seed and woos the owner's girlfriend by mimicking his voice and giving her a feather massage. "Pygmalion" won the Eighth Grade Short Story Contest and Mr. Krueger posted it for everyone to read. Brian Ching and Speedy Naki congratulated me and Debbie told me she didn't know I could write.

"That Pygmalion story was neato!" Lucy said between classes out at the lockers. She wore a buckskin cowboy jacket with frills, denims, and cowboy boots.

"Thanks, Lucy."

"You can give me a feather massage anytime, Jeff."

"Do you have a feather?"

"No, but I bet I can find one at the carnival."

I liked Lucy but I hated it when girls fawned over me. It was too easy and made her less foxy. I had to change the subject. "Your father suspended me," I said.

"I know," she replied, "he told me all about it."

"Did you tell him he was wrong to do that?"

"How could I? You did cut class, Jeffrey Gill."

"Are you Punahou's next principal?" I asked her.

"No."

"Anyway, it wigged out my father."

"Sorry. But my Dad was just doing his job. I can ask him to apologize if you want."

The idea of Dr. Seville apologizing to an eighth grader was ludicrous. I imagined sitting in Seville's chair wearing a suit and tie and using the intercom to tell Miss Patton to send Seville in. Seville entered with a sheepish expression wearing a beanie cap on his head and shorts held up by suspenders. "I'm so sorry, Master Gill," he said, "it will never happen again." "See that it doesn't, kid," I replied, "and get rid of that damn beanie cap." I chuckled.

"What's so funny?" Lucy asked.

"Oh, nothing."

"Go on. Spill the beans, Jeff."

"You're just so goofy sometimes, Lucy."

She frowned. "Does this mean you're not asking me to the carnival?"

"I already asked Debbie Mills," I lied.

"Well," Lucy huffed, "for your information, Jeffrey Gill, I wouldn't go with you if you were the last boy in the state of Hawaii."

The bell rang for the next period and Lucy stomped off down the corridor.

*   *   *

Winning the short story contest made me feel as though I was back at Star of the Sea, where awards and honors came easier. But, despite winning the contest, my overall grade in English was a C-plus. I hated most of the assignments Mr. Krueger gave us. He told us to make something to honor the memory of Mark Twain and I tried carving a pipe out of a corncob but the cob crumbled. Then the tiny Huck Finn raft I made out of toothpicks disintegrated on the way to school.

"You're a tough guy to grade," Mr. Krueger told me after class. "You get As in all my writing assignments but don't bother to turn in your arts and crafts projects."

"I hate arts and crafts," I said.

"It's a good thing you enjoy writing," Mr. Krueger said, "otherwise, I'd have to flunk you."

Mr. Krueger loaned me a dogeared copy of *The Norton Anthology of Poetry* and I read poems by Ginsberg and Ferlinghetti. I read lines from "Howl" to my father and he said Ginsberg was ready for the loony bin.

I started buying kits and building model airplanes. Zeros, Mustangs, Spitfires, and Stukas hung from my ceiling on lines of catgut. My other hobby was raising monarch butterflies. I'd found a milkweed tree loaded with caterpillars during my summer on Moloka'i—I smuggled the best leaves and the healthiest caterpillars to Honolulu in Gramma's old pickle jars. I set up Caterpillar Town in an open terrarium. The caterpillars fattened up on the leaves and most left Caterpillar Town to build their chrysalises. They would find unusual places to suspend their bodies and begin their metamorphoses—on a hanger in the closet, on the lampshade, on the wing of a plane. I liked butterflies because of their ability to transform and fly away. I was determined to see them safely through the chrysalis stage and release them into the wild when they flapped their wings dry.

*   *   *

Our mother looked worried after seeing our report cards. She said we couldn't show them to our father unless he was in a good mood. But he found out on his own because BeeBe's son went to Punahou and BeeBe bragged incessantly at the firm about his boy's grades and how he was "Harvard material."

My father cornered me in the kitchen when he got home from work. "Why didn't you show me your report card?" he asked.

"I forgot."

"Bullshit. You've got something to hide."

My mother walked in. "Who's got something to hide?" she asked.

"Did the boys show you their report cards?"

"No, Dear."

"Go get your report card now, Jeffrey," my father said.

I retreated to my room and pulled *Tom Swift and the Visitor from Planet X* off the bookshelf—my report card was behind the front cover. I returned to the kitchen and handed my father a dossier where each page was a summary of quarterly grades for a subject and included teacher comments. A separate page revealed class rank. My father's expression turned from disappointment to disgust.

"More god damn Cs," he said leafing through the pages.

"C-plus," I said.

"That's passing," my mother said.

"Passing, my ass."

"At least it's not a D, " my mother responded. She always ran interference for us because she hadn't done well in school either. She felt that developing charm and an appreciation for the arts was what really mattered.

My father read the teacher comments after balling me out about my grades. "Mr. Strombeck says you're 'reserved in response,' Jeffrey. Why the hell don't you speak up?"

"I'll try harder."

"Know what your problem is?"

"What?"

"You've gotta lazy streak a mile wide."

"I've seen him studying," said my mother.

"I'm sick of paying all that money so he can be a stupe."

Ben opened the front door and it was his turn. He wore his paisley shirt and bellbottoms and, after he retrieved his report card, he handed it to my father with a sheepish expression. Ben hardly studied. He spent most

of his Study Hall time flirting with Monica Apianni, a girl
with raven hair and a smile so beautiful she made
everything seem right with the universe. My father yelled
at Ben for getting a C-minus in Home Economics and recited
Mrs. Goodhue's critique of Ben's culinary talents: "Made
green pancakes and spit in the syrup."

Wait until he sees Juicy's grade in Algebra, I thought.
I retreated to my room. A monarch had hatched and it was
trapped between my louvered window and the screen. I
pushed the screen open—the butterfly fluttered to a lemon
tree and rested on a leaf before flying off. I pretended it
would find Debbie. I imagined her in an emerald dress
with my orange butterfly flying around her.

*   *   *

The Punahou Carnival arrived and I was riding the
Infinity Swing on lower field when I saw Debbie with
Wayne. He had his arm around her waist and they were
sharing a cotton candy. I was ten feet in the air on a swing
attached by chains to a giant rotating wheel. I wanted to
shout something cool but couldn't think of anything as I
circled above them. I spit and it hit Wayne in the face.
Wayne wiped his face and spotted me swinging by.

"You're dead, Squirt!" he said. He handed Debbie
the cotton candy and stationed himself at the exit.

The ride slowed down and I unbuckled the seat belt
while we were still moving. I jumped off and hit the ground
running.

"Stop!" a carny said.

I hurdled a low chain-link fence surrounding the ride

and Wayne chased me. I ran for the midway. I darted past the shooting gallery and the malasada booth. Wayne bumped into a woman carrying a bag of malasadas and the malasadas went flying. I ducked behind a monkeypod tree and cut through the line at the meat sticks booth.

"Hey, Peanut!" Ben said. He was eating meat sticks with Monica in front of the saimin booth.

"Who's Peanut?" asked Monica.

"My doofus brother," Ben replied.

Wayne stood in the midway looking down the row of game booths. He shifted his attention to the food booths. He spotted me and I scooted past the corn booth and the game arcade. The Twinkies were firing .22 rifles in the shooting gallery and the smell of burnt powder made me run faster. I darted past a booth where a crowd had gathered to watch girls throw wet blobs of blue and green cornstarch at Mr. Tenant—he'd been imprisoned in a wooden box with only his head sticking out. I saw the open flap of the monstrous white elephant tent and ran in. I hid behind a display of toasters, monkeypod bowls, and koa platters. I crept into the book section and most of the books were still boxed. I spotted Lucy pulling a bowler hat off a Styrofoam head. She put it on and used the mirror in her compact to check herself out.

"Whacha doing, Lucy?" I asked.

"None of your beeswax."

"Your Dad would look cool in that hat."

"Get lost, Jeffrey Gill."

"Can I buy you a malasada?"

Lucy slipped her compact into her purse and put the hat back on the Styrofoam head. "Thought you were taking Miss Hot Stuff to the carnival?"

"I didn't really ask her."

"How come?"

"She's going steady with Wayne Braswell."

"Debbie doesn't have very good taste, does she?"

"No."

"Okay, let's go," said Lucy, "but I'm not going steady with you, no matter how much you beg."

We made our way over to the opening in the tent and Wayne stood in our way.

"We got business to settle, Squirt," Wayne said.

"I'm busy," I replied.

"If you try anything funny, Wayne Braswell," Lucy warned, "I'll make my father expel you."

Wayne stuck his tongue out at Lucy. "I'll see you in school, Squirt," he said, "see you real soon."

"By the way, creepo," Lucy said, "where's Debbie?"

"Hot damn," Wayne replied and dashed out of the tent.

"Now," Lucy told me, "let's go get those malasadas."

*   *   *

I spent over an hour at Longs Drugs in Kahala Mall trying to find a cool Valentine's Day card for Debbie. I finally settled on a card with two cats cuddling but I was too shy to put it on her desk in Study Hall the next morning. Nobody was exchanging cards and suddenly giving a Valentine seemed mushy and uncool. The bell rang and

Debbie glided out. I saw her at Dole Cafeteria but Wayne was with her. I saw her after school on the hill outside Bishop Hall and watched until a white VW Bug pulled up and she jogged down to meet it. I ran after her. A blonde lady was behind the wheel.

"Debbie," I said, "Debbie Mills!"

Debbie turned around and waited for me.

"Hi, Jeff," she said sweeping a strand of blonde hair out of her eyes. She wore a green muumuu with a flower print and the fabric hugged the curves of her body. She held her books in one hand and a stack of Valentines was wedged between the pages of her geography textbook. I liked how the sun lit up her hair and the way her smile wrinkled the corners of her mouth.

"This is for you," I said handing her the card.

"Far-out," she said. "Mind if I open it later?"

"No. Not at all."

She opened her textbook, placed my card on the bottom of the others, and snapped the book shut. "How old are you anyway?" she asked.

"Thirteen."

"You look way younger."

"I do?"

She nodded. "You look about ten or eleven."

"But I'll be fourteen in September."

"Come on, Deb," the blonde lady said from inside the car, "say goodbye to Romeo. We don't got all day."

Debbie opened the door and climbed in. "See ya."

"Aloha," I answered.

They headed off down Palm Drive. The muffler rattled when the blonde lady shifted gears. She hung a right on Wilder Avenue and the Bug was gone. I felt good for finally giving Debbie the card but bad too because she hadn't given me one. "Aloha," I mumbled, "what a dense thing to say."

                    *   *   *

I wanted to make myself look older for Debbie. I was too young to grow a moustache or sideburns to disguise my baby face. I went on a diet so my face would appear less chubby. I'd heard that the sun and frowning gave you wrinkles so I spent my weekend sunning my face and frowning at the sky. Cigarettes were supposed to age you but I nearly choked to death after my first puff off a lipstick-stained Virginia Slim I'd found in the gutter. I put on one of my mother's wigs to see if I'd look older with long hair but I resembled a Hawaiian Shirley Temple. After a week of trying to age myself, I looked even younger.

"Why do I have to look so young?" I asked my mother.

"Because you are young," she answered.

"A girl at school thinks I look ten."

"Why, you don't look that young. Who is this girl?"

"Just someone."

"Someday," she said, "you'll be glad you have a baby face."

                    *   *   *

Eighth grade ended when the mythic stream shifted its subterranean path and pooled beneath Bishop Hall. The building moaned during my History class and the Diamond Head side sank six feet. Fire alarms sounded and everyone evacuated. We all congregated on middle field. Bishop Hall's roof slanted at a thirty-degree angle and, after ten minutes, the building groaned. Dr. Seville ordered everyone back. Teachers, students, and administrators retreated as the Diamond Head side sank another six feet.

"Abandon ship," I said and got a few laughs.

"There goes the *Titanic*," a boy called out.

Laughter spread through the crowd. The boy's voice sounded familiar. I turned around—it was Wayne. His right arm rested on Debbie's shoulder. Debbie had her arm around his waist and she looked up at him as if he'd just delivered The Gettysburg Address.

Dr. Seville gave us the last three weeks off because Punahou didn't want to get sued in case a student got sucked down into the earth. My father was convinced we'd been suspended again and he phoned Dr. Seville just to make sure. Yearbooks arrived in mailers that summer without signatures or messages. Junior high was history but I wasn't happy. The girl I loved barely knew I existed and I would have to wait an entire summer before seeing her again.

HIGH SCHOOL

A three-ton lava stone stood at Punahou's main entrance on the corner of Wilder Avenue and Punahou Street. The stone had been used by Hawaiians to bless expectant mothers and to endow newborns with wisdom and strength. The school used cement to patch fissures in the lava. The stone was splattered with drops of cement and a bronze plaque riveted to it read: "Punahou School, Founded 1841."

The buildings on the high school side of campus were a mixture of old and new, everything from coral stone Old School Hall to cement Cooke Library with its copper roof and tinted windows. There were two auditoriums, a gym, a dozen tennis courts, three large fields, a clay track, two Olympic pools, an observatory, and a radio station. The campus was a landscaped masterpiece of coconut trees, date palms, banyans, paper birches, and the revered halas. Tropical gardens featured bamboo, jasmine, red ginger, and bird of paradise. Flowering trees included plumeria, jacaranda, and royal poinciana. Trade winds kept the campus cool. Upperclass couples held hands and strolled through lush acres like 20th Century Adams and Eves. The grounds were maintained by a troop of fastidious gardeners who worked under the watchful eye of Mr. Tanaka, a vet who'd received the Purple Heart fighting for the Army's 442nd Division in the Argonne Forest. Mr. Tanaka patrolled the campus from dawn to dusk in his Chevy truck.

On my first day, I felt as if I'd passed through the turnstiles at Disneyland. Punahou Academy was a village of three thousand teenagers and adults. Juniors and seniors organized antiwar rallies. Students played guitars at noon. A gable clock at Cooke Hall chimed the hour. I felt lost in the rush of activity. My classmates felt lost too. The cliques that defined our class in junior high blurred in a whirlwind of councils, committees, organizations, associations, choirs, choruses, ensembles, bands, crews, and teams. It was almost like starting all over again at a new school because the terrain was different, freshmen were on the bottom rung, and twenty new freshmen had joined our ranks.

"Stay away from seniors," Lucy warned me, "especially at high noon."

"How come?" I asked.

"They make freshmen carry their lunch trays."

"What if I refuse?"

"You can't," she claimed, "it's the law."

All I wanted to do was to find Debbie—she wasn't in any of my classes and I had yet to see her on campus.

*   *   *

An assembly was held in the gym on the first Friday
and freshmen sat together in the bleachers. Ben and Wayne
were a few rows down from me. I sat beside Lucy; things
had cooled between us but we were still friends. I couldn't
find Debbie in the crowd and I was surprised she wasn't
with Wayne. The Punahou cheerleaders charged out in
blue and yellow uniforms. "Go, Buff 'n' Blue!" they shouted
through blue cardboard megaphones. After lots of skirt
twirling, synchronized kicks, and building a human
pyramid, the cheerleaders led us in the singing of "Oahu`a,"
the school anthem. Two husky boys carried out a podium
and set it down on the gym floor. The class deans delivered
short speeches, including Dean McQueen, our dean for the
next four years. We received a welcoming message from
President Young, a short man with shiny black hair, gambler
eyes, and a bushy moustache. Young's ancestors had made
a fortune buying and selling land after helping overthrow
Queen Lili'uokalani in 1893.

"Students must do their part," Young said solemnly,
"to maintain the integrity and high standards of our
institution."

Wayne slipped a hand under his shirt, nestled it in
his pit, and cranked his arm up and down. Laughter spread
through the crowd when Young's speech was interrupted
by the sound of farts.

*   *   *

I was eating a mahimahi sandwich at the snack shop
and trying my best to avoid seniors when Ben tapped me

on the shoulder. "Your li'l Debbie's flown the coop," he said.

"She broke up with Wayne?" I asked.

"She split for the Lone Star State."

"Where's that?"

"Texas, doofus."

"Why would she go there?"

"Her Dad's in the military," Ben said. "Wayne's going to write her."

"Can I have her address?"

"You'll have to ask Wayne."

Except for that Valentine's moment outside Bishop Hall, Debbie didn't really know I liked her. I had always held out hope she would tire of Wayne and give me a chance. Wayne chuckled when I asked for her address. I asked a second time and he said, "I wouldn't do this for just any Joe Blow," and scrawled down an address in my spiral notebook. I sent off a quick letter and it was returned with the apologies of the clerk at the Texas Supreme Court. For me, Debbie became synonymous with Texas. Whenever the Lone Star State came up in the news or conversation, I thought about her. I looked for her whenever the Dallas Cowboys played home games on TV; Ben pointed out blonde girls in Texas Stadium and whined, "Oh, Jeffrey, I miss you so."

POI DOGS

I talked my father into putting up a basketball net over the garage when he saw my grades slipping in PE. He'd been procrastinating because he thought the ball would bounce on the roof and snap the shakes. He opened his trunk on a Friday after work and it was stuffed with basketball gear—an official NBA ball, a white plywood backboard, an orange rim, and a white nylon net. I helped him bolt down support beams to the roof, attach mounting brackets, and hang the backboard.

My father held the tape measure against the rim and dangled the end down to me. "How high's it gotta be?" he asked.

I grabbed the tape and pinned it to the ground. "Ten feet."

"How 'bout nine feet, nine inches?"

"That's not official."

"Okay," he said tinkering with the rim, "wouldn't

wanna break the rules."

* * *

I shot baskets after school. Ben couldn't understand how throwing a ball in a hoop was so exciting. My father took a few shots when he got home from work and then went inside for his nap. The ball echoed off the asphalt as I dribbled out to the hala tree on the far side of the driveway. I drove to the basket and fired a fallaway jumper at the baseline—the ball flew between the branches of the dragon tree and bounced off the rim. I grabbed the rebound, dribbled to the crack in the asphalt, and launched a bomb that found the net. My skin glowed in the late afternoon light and my arms and legs ached from shooting jump shots and going high for rebounds. I played past dusk, until the first planets and stars burned through the purple sky. Within two weeks I could dribble the ball between my legs, make jumpers from twenty feet out, and shoot foul shots with some consistency. I glided around a court of imaginary challengers and shot rainbows over the outstretched arms of giants to eke out last second victories. I played life or death matches until the yellow light from the dining room spilled over the blacktop and my mother called, "Time to set the table, Jeffrey."

* * *

Mr. Farley was my PE coach. He was hapa haole and in his early thirties. The Punahou girls liked him because of his boyish good looks. He always wore sunglasses and shorts around campus and had modeled for Wren's Men's Store at Kahala Mall. "Eye candy," said

Cecily Hess. Farley believed that the best way for boys to develop character and a love for sports was by putting them in head-to-head competition. He taught us rudimentary skills like dribbling and the bank shot and broke our class into teams. I'd impressed him enough with my skills in a scrimmage for him to pick me as one of the eight team captains. Ben was in the class but Farley didn't pick him because Ben's dislike for the game was obvious. Farley ordered each captain to draft four teammates out of the pool of PE students. I knew Ben wouldn't hold it against me if I didn't select him. I picked Speedy Naki and Brian Ching, boys who made up for their lack of height with quickness and tenacity. I took Hugh O'Malley for his baseline jumper and George Fujioka because I thought of him as a diamond in the rough. We named our team "the Poi Dogs." We had to face the seven other teams in a round robin tournament over the course of three weeks. The championship game would match the two teams with the most wins.

The Poi Dogs were scheduled to play the Fantastic Five in the first round of the tourney. Wayne was their captain and his teammates were haoles who all belonged to the Outrigger Canoe Club. Brad Cooper, a freckle-faced kid with a blond Afro, was one of Wayne's forwards. Cooper had told me I was a "short mongrel" in the Boys' Locker Room when we were changing into our school-issued khaki shorts and white tees.

Four small courts ran the width of the gym and three games were already in progress when we took the floor against the Fantastic Five. Three other PE teachers were there to help ref the games. I could smell the sweat from the years of boys and girls playing in the gym. I got worried watching the Fantastic Five shoot at the far court—nearly every shot went in. I spotted Wesley Easton dribbling the ball like a pro and zigzagging around the key. Wesley was a sprinter on the track team and he'd just placed second in the state finals.

"Shirts or skins?" Farley asked me.

"Skins."

Farley nodded. A silver whistle was attached to a loop of blue rope around his neck. "Poi Dogs," he said, "take off your shirts."

I pulled off my tee and tossed it out of bounds.

"Why'd you make us skins?" George Fujioka asked me.

"What's wrong with that?"

George looked around the gym before pulling his tee over his head and balling it up. "I hate showing my chest," he admitted and threw his tee into the first row of the bleachers. His skin was white and he had no body hair. Some of the football players called him "Hotel Street mahu" because of his gentle nature. He crossed his arms and held them high to hide his chest, like a wizard preparing to cast a spell.

Farley walked to center court holding the ball and both teams took up positions around him. Wayne volunteered to jump for the Fantastic Five. Nobody on my team stepped forward to jump.

"Who's jumping, Poi Dogs?" asked Farley.

Wayne chuckled. "Poi Chickens is more like it."

"I'm jumping," I said and stood opposite Wayne. He was taller than Ben.

"I own this floor, Squirt," Wayne said.

Farley put his whistle in his mouth. Wayne crouched down and so did I. The whistle sounded the instant the ball went up. When the ball came down, Wayne batted it over to Cooper. Cooper zipped past George, sprinted to the basket, and laid the ball in.

"Nice play, Coop," Wesley said.

I waved my hand and Hugh inbounded the ball to me. My sneakers squeaked against the gym floor as I dribbled toward the opposite basket. It all felt like a dream, with me bouncing the ball off the parquet floor and my teammates fighting for positions. The Twinkie twins were stationed at the top of the key—they were Wayne's height and, when they held up their arms, I had trouble seeing the basket. This was a lot different than playing imaginary games out on the blacktop. Wayne came up flailing his arms and said, "Shoot, Squirt, shoot!" I panicked and tossed the ball in the direction of Speedy. Coop intercepted my pass and scored with me and Brian trailing after him.

"Way to swoop, Coop!" Wayne laughed.

I inbounded the ball to Brian and he dribbled down to the top of the key. He faked a pass to George and hit a wide open Speedy. Speedy made a bold move to the basket but the Twinkies converged and one swatted away his shot. Coop grabbed the loose ball and tossed it downcourt to

Wesley for a fast break basket.

"Yee-ha!" said Wayne.

That's how the game went for the most part. Whenever I got in close and attempted a shot, Wayne or a Twinkie was there to bat it away. When I tried anything long distance, the ball either missed the rim entirely or bounced off the backboard and fell into the waiting arms of Wayne. I turned the ball over once for traveling and twice for dribbling out of bounds. Hugh sunk a few baseline jumpers, Speedy got a drive to fall, and I sunk two foul shots after Wayne sent me flying when he slammed into me under the net. When Farley blew the final whistle, the score was 35 to 12 in favor of the Fantastic Five.

"We suck," George said pulling his tee over his head.

We all watched the Fantastic Five congratulate one another at midcourt as if they'd just won the NBA Finals. Hugh kicked the basketball and it landed halfway up in the bleachers. Brian and Speedy held their heads low, like scolded mutts.

"We'll get better," I said.

"How?" Brian asked me.

"Practice."

Speedy frowned. "I gotta work after school."

I felt bad for Speedy. He'd lost his football scholarship when he got cut from the team. He was from the Homesteads in Nanakuli and didn't want to become a construction worker like his father. "How 'bout we practice every day before we eat lunch?" I asked Speedy.

He thought about it for a moment. "I can do that."

George nodded. "Bet we still suck."

*   *   *

The Poi Dogs met at noon the next day in the gym.
I'd checked out a ball from the PE Office and I dribbled it
over the parquet floor before passing it to Hugh. The gym
was deserted except for two girls in shorts hitting a
volleyball back and forth. One was Lucy and the other
was Dawn Yamashita, a tall Japanese girl who'd placed
second in Miss Teenage Hawaii.

"Hi, Jeff," Lucy said.

"Howz it, Lucy," I answered. "Getting in some extra
practice?"

Lucy crouched down and hit the volleyball back to
Dawn with the heels of her palms. "We play Kam this
Saturday," she replied.

"Still dating that senior?"

Lucy returned the ball. "Arnold dumped me after
he got into USC."

"I'm sorry, Lucy."

Lucy missed a return and blamed me for distracting
her. I walked to the far side of the gym with the Poi Dogs
and we played in our school clothes. I'd found a book in
Cooke Library outlining some basic offensive plays and we
tried the Give and Go, the Backdoor, and the Inside
Handoff. I made Hugh our center because he was the
tallest—he had his Irish father's height and his Chinese
mother's features. Speedy and Brian were guards and
George and I were forwards. We were miserably out of
sync and I passed the ball out of bounds instead of hitting

Speedy when he cut to the basket. Hugh missed every baseline jumper he took and Speedy fumbled two passes from George. I slipped on the parquet floor in my flip-flops and fell hard. Only Brian seemed to have any skill and grace as he dribbled the ball in figure eights around us. George tripped on a volleyball that had rolled onto the court. Brian passed to Hugh. Hugh dribbled clumsily to the baseline and put up a shot that flew four feet over the rim.

"That Lucy Seville's so fine," Hugh decided.

"We gotta learn to concentrate," I reminded him.

"Think I sprained something," Hugh said inspecting his hand.

"I can't get over it," said George.

"Can't get over what?" I asked.

"How much we suck," George replied.

*   *   *

The Geckos were the second team to challenge us in the tourney. I figured we could beat them because most of the Geckos were either Surfers or Druggies. Ben was on their team and he didn't care if they won or lost—he was sitting in the bleachers reading *Car and Driver Magazine* when I entered the gym. The Geckos practiced on their side of the court and only a few shots were falling. One Gecko played in swim trunks and talked about the waves on the North Shore. "Gnarly barrels," he said.

"Shirts or skins?" Farley asked me.

"Shirts."

"We're going to get clobbered," said George, "but at

least we'll lose with our shirts on." He'd spent the weekend under his mother's sunlamp and now his skin was pink instead of white.

Farley told Ben to quit reading, take off his shirt, and get on the court. Ben strolled shirtless to midcourt and watched indifferently as the two teams converged. Farley blew the whistle and the ball was in the air. Hugh tipped the ball into Ben's hands. Ben bounced the ball awkwardly, double dribbled, and turned it over to us. I moved the ball downcourt, passed it to Hugh on the baseline, and he put up a shot that bounced high off the rim. Ben grabbed the rebound, threw the basketball like a football to a teammate streaking for the basket, and the Geckos scored the game's first points. Our offense was practically nonexistent for the next ten minutes. Speedy couldn't get one of his underhand layups to fall and George and Hugh couldn't hit from the floor. A Gecko stole the ball from Brian and sprinted for an easy bucket. "Radical!" cheered his teammate. I made one of two foul shots after getting hammered trying a reverse layup. The Geckos played great man-to-man defense and George got flustered handling the ball in the backcourt. George threw up a prayer from downtown—surprisingly, the ball swished through the net. I stole the inbounds pass and banked the ball off the glass to score for the Poi Dogs. Hugh hit a fallaway jumper. But after that burst, our offense went cold. Speedy fell on a drive to the basket, hurt his ankle, and started to hobble. I tried a hook shot that missed the rim entirely and the ball dropped into Ben's hands. Ben passed the ball all the way downcourt to an open Gecko who scored. It seemed like one fast break opportunity after another for the Geckos. We lost our second game by seven points.

"See?" said George. "We suck, we really do."

"At least we're getting closer," I told him.

"Closer," Speedy replied limping to the sideline, "but no cigar."

                    *   *   *

We continued practicing at lunchtime. I told everyone to wear running shoes or sneakers instead of flip-flops. Speedy's ankle got better but he still couldn't go full speed. I coached us through as best I could and one day we just goofed off and took turns shooting. We found out George was deadly with a two-hand set shot from five feet behind the charity stripe and Brian surprised us with the accuracy of his passes. I showed them how to do a reverse layup off the glass and we worked on our man-to-man defense.

                    *   *   *

I felt more confident when we challenged the Running Buddhas, an all-Asian team of great shooters and superb ball handlers. Hugh towered over their center on the opening jump. Farley tossed the ball up and Hugh knocked it over to me—I drove the length of the floor and hit a jumper at the top of the key. It was the first time the Poi Dogs had ever led in a game and that inspired us. The Running Buddhas liked a quick game with lots of turnovers but we countered with good defense and consistent rebounding. I slowed the game down by setting up a four corners offense and we passed the ball around for minutes on end, until one of us broke unexpectedly for the basket and scored an easy layup. That strategy backfired when a Running Buddha intercepted one of my passes, but overall it lulled our opponents into complacency. The whistle sounded and the Poi Dogs had won by five points.

*   *   *

Winning that first game galvanized us as a team. We beat the Heebie Jeebies after being behind early and repeated that performance against the Mango Heads. Brian spurred us on with his never-say-die attitude and great passing. George got so confident with his set shot that he could hit it more than half the time. Hugh remained our baseline specialist. Speedy's ankle healed and he was a constant threat to cut to the hoop and score. I was a freelancer, sometimes going in low to hit with a hook, other times making shots from the perimeter. In our sixth game, we squeaked out a victory over highly favored Mochi Crunch thanks to Speedy's steal of an errant pass in the final minute. We finished the tourney with an offensive blitz that stunned the Mahimahis by fifteen points and that moved us up to second place overall in the rankings behind the undefeated Fantastic Five.

Farley tallied up all the wins and losses on a sheet attached to his clipboard. "Fantastic Five against the Poi Dogs for the championship on Friday," he announced.

"Already beat 'em once, coach," said Coop.

"You'll have to beat 'em again," said Farley.

Wayne smirked. "Poi Chickens are dead meat."

* * *

It was the last day of basketball and time for the championship. PE students not participating in the game didn't have to suit up but they did have to watch from the bleachers. I walked in with the Poi Dogs. The players for the Fantastic Five wore teal jerseys with "The Fantastic Five" embroidered in gold on their breast pockets. Wayne passed the ball to Coop and he fired a jumper that swished through the net. The Twinkies shot bank shots off the glass while Wesley dribbled the ball in circles.

"Where'd they get the jerseys?" I asked Mr. Farley.

"Coop's father owns Crazy Shirts," he answered.

Speedy glared downcourt. "Jerseys won't help those mahus win."

"At least we don't have to be skins," said George. His skin was red and peeling because he'd overdone it with his mother's sunlamp.

The game would be played the length of the gym instead of its width and I was glad I'd worked bleacher running into our practices to improve stamina. I shot at our basket with the Poi Dogs. Brian fed Hugh and Hugh hit from the baseline. Speedy cut to the basket and tossed up an underhand roller that went in. Boys in the bleachers from Mochi Crunch said, "Woof, woof!" Ben was camped on the highest row of the bleachers with his back pressed against the gym wall.

I thought about how the Poi Dogs had started out as the worst team in the tourney but fought back to become

second best. It made me think that anything was possible
if you kept trying and believed in yourself and your
teammates. I realized luck had something to do with it too
but maybe a connection existed between luck and not
quitting. We'd spent our last two practices learning a zone
called "Thirty Defense," one that started out man-to-man
but switched to double-teams to confuse ball handlers. I
thought it was a good idea to have a surprise for the
Fantastic Five. I sunk a hook shot and passed the ball out
to Speedy—he drove toward the basket and, when he
elevated for the rim, he seemed suspended in air.

The whistle blew. "Let's play ball!" Farley said.

Wayne won the tip-off against Hugh and a Twinkie
hit a jumper for the Fantastic Five to begin the scoring. I
took the inbounds pass from Brian and dribbled down the
court. I passed it to Hugh on the wing. Hugh took a shot
from beyond his range and Coop snatched the rebound.
The Fantastic Five scored on their next possession when
Wesley drove through the paint and hit a runner. George
scored our first points by hitting a bomb from downtown
and Hugh grabbed his own rebound off a missed shot and
put it back in. Brian got fouled and he made both of his
shots. Speedy was a demon on the court—he got two early
steals and scored uncontested layups. "Woof, woof!" I
heard from the bleachers. The Fantastic Five seemed rattled
by Speedy's quickness so they put Wesley on him to negate
his speed. Wesley was able to slow Speedy down but his
focus on defense hurt him offensively. George hit another
set shot from behind the key and I sunk a fallaway jumper

after rebounding a miss by a Twinkie. The Fantastic Five countered with buckets by Wayne and Coop. The half ended with the Poi Dogs leading by three points.

"We gotta build a bigger lead," I told the Poi Dogs as we huddled along the sidelines.

"I'm stoked we're ahead at all," said Hugh, "after that beating we took the first time."

"We're not the same team," Speedy replied.

"Yeah," said George, "we hardly suck at all."

We got the ball first in the second half and George hit his two-hand set shot to increase our lead. We traded buckets with the Fantastic Five for the first ten minutes. A Twinkie elbowed me in the cheek when I tried dribbling past him and I lost the ball to his twin. The twin missed his shot and I grabbed the rebound and headed downcourt. This time I didn't dribble past the Twinkie who'd elbowed me—I ran into him on purpose and sent him flying across the parquet floor.

"Flagrant!" said Wayne.

The whistle blew. "Two shots," said Farley.

The Twinkie made one of two foul shots. In the next five minutes Wayne hurt us with ten straight points— everything he threw up either swished through the net or bounced off the backboard and angled in for the score. Our lead was gone. The Fantastic Five dominated us on defense by keeping the Twinkies inside the key to bat away shots and to snatch rebounds. Wesley sailed up to block my layup on a breakaway. Our only points came from Hugh's baseline jumpers and Speedy's quick hands and drives to the basket. We were losing by eight points with the game winding down. Brian fed Speedy and Speedy put up a teardrop that just cleared the outstretched hand of a Twinkie to score. Coop missed a jumper and I got the rebound. I dribbled for their unprotected net but Wesley trapped me on the baseline. I stopped, pivoted with my left foot, and accidentally dragged it.

The whistle blew. "Traveling!" Farley said.

"It's okay," Brian told me, "settle down, Jeff. We've still got time."

"Thirty Defense!" I called and the Poi Dogs nodded.

Wayne inbounded the ball to Coop. Coop dribbled upcourt and Hugh picked him up. When Coop got to the perimeter, Speedy quit guarding Wesley and double-teamed Coop. Coop got confused, looked around for help, and Hugh knocked the ball away. Speedy grabbed the loose ball, ran downcourt, and put the ball in the net.

"Woof, woof!" cheered the boys in the bleachers.

"Way to hustle, Speedy," I said.

We continued playing Thirty Defense. Hugh and George double-teamed Wayne. Wayne threw a crosscourt pass to Wesley that I intercepted and took all the way for a basket.

We had less than a minute to play and Wayne slowed the game down by keeping Coop close and playing keep away when we double-teamed. They didn't even bother dribbling and kept the ball chest level. I tried poking the ball away from Wayne and he elbowed me in the ribs before passing it back to Coop. Brian and Speedy both teamed up on Coop and a Twinkie slipped through our defense and waved for the ball under the basket. Coop threw the ball hard and the Twinkie fumbled it out of bounds.

"Fifteen seconds!" said Farley.

I looked up at the scoreboard and we were down by one basket. Hugh inbounded the ball to Brian while Speedy raced toward the key with Wesley on his heels. Brian threw me the ball at midcourt. I dribbled past the outstretched hands of Coop and headed for the net. Wayne was waiting for me in the paint. I turned my back to him and dug my shoulder into his chest. I quit dribbling, did a head fake, and Wayne went up to block my shot. But I didn't shoot. Wayne bumped me on his way down—I angled my body under the net and tried a reverse layup with my left hand off the glass. The ball bounced off the backboard, rolled around the rim, and fell in as time expired.

Farley blew his whistle. "That counts and there's a foul!"

"No!" said Wayne.

"One shot," Farley said.

I stood at the charity stripe and bounced the ball. Even if I missed we'd go to overtime. My heart pounded. Sweat from my forehead trickled down into my eyes. I bounced the ball. I quit bouncing and held the ball with both hands while I studied the basket. The rim didn't seem far away. Not far at all. I bent at the knees, came up with the ball, and let it go. The ball hit the side of the rim, rolled off, and Wayne snagged the rebound.

The whistle blew. "Lane violation!" Farley said

pointing at Wayne.

"You've gotta be fuckin' kidding," Wayne mumbled.

"Did you just swear at me, Wayne?" asked Farley.

"No, Mr. Farley."

"Give Jeff the ball."

Wayne tossed me the ball and returned to his lane.

"One shot," Farley said.

This time I wanted to take a shot without thinking about it. I shifted the weight of the ball to my left hand and bent at the knees. I cocked my wrist and launched my second chance shot. The ball hit the back of the rim, bounced straight up, and fell into the net.

"Poi Dogs win," Farley announced, "the Poi Dogs are champs!"

The boys charged down from the bleachers to congratulate us. "Radical game!" cheered a Gecko. Two boys from Mochi Crunch said Speedy deserved to be the MVP of the tourney. Ben told me I was ready for the NBA. Wayne just stood in his lane staring at me in disbelief.

THE ENCHANTRESS

Kainalu Stream marked the eastern boundary of Hale Kia, Gramma's ranch on Moloka'i. The stream was congested with refrigerators, stoves, washers, and dryers. Chipper Daniels, Gramma's ex, had started the practice of tossing in busted appliances after his house burned to the ground. I didn't mind because the water was murky and I liked marking a good summer fishing spot in relation to a shiny surface. Someone had tried sinking a DeSoto but the surging waters from a monsoon rolled the car down to the shore.

A sand bar formed at the stream's mouth in dry weather. During hard rains, water dammed up behind the sand bar until the swollen stream broke through. Mercury Duva and his brother Dodge rode paipo boards from deep in the valley out to the harbor—the raging water exposed the appliances but the boys steered clear of them the way kayakers avoid boulders going down the rapids.

Fresh water from Kainalu Stream had discouraged coral growth offshore and created a natural harbor. Legend had it that the harbor had been the home of the Mo'o Ali'i, the shark god who guarded the coast; a Tahitian sea captain harpooned the Mo'o Ali'i when it approached his ship and the Hawaiians buried their god beside a waterfall. Gramma said the Mo'o Ali'i's ghost led the 'O'io Marchers down from the mountain at night to fish.

*   *   *

The Kristofersons owned a cottage five miles east of Hale Kia. Sometimes they boated over from Honolulu and dropped anchor in the harbor. Mr. and Mrs. Kristoferson had three girls and a boy. Lisa and Laverne were twins. All the Kristofersons were blonde. Mr. Kristoferson had made a killing in the insurance business after spending a decade as plant manager for Bumble Bee Tuna. He had a good build, a great tan, and a happy-go-lucky nature.

Ben and I called Chipper "uncle" and so did the Kristoferson children. They rarely visited him on their own because he didn't like kids dropping by. Lisa and Laverne hiked to Hale Kia not to see their uncle but to ride our horses. Ben and I saddled Sparkling Eyes and Jetty in the morning so the girls could ride through the ironwood forest and along the beach.

Mrs. Kristoferson was Chipper's niece. I felt bad knowing she'd see how he lived when she brought him supplies. Chipper had told me about waking during flash floods to find his floor underwater and the walls crawling with black worms, snails, and centipedes. He'd turned

down Mr. Kristoferson's offer to build a house on stilts
because Gramma had only given him a life estate. His shack
was in a constant state of repair. Chipper scoured the shore
every morning for lumber and sheets of plywood. Some of
the wood his friend Moki had used to build the shack was
maple and that attracted a colony of termites. Chipper had
been forced to tear down an entire wall, one termite-infested
plank at a time.

Gramma backed her International Scout up to the
dump every Tuesday to unload garbage. Ben and I tossed
Hefty bags fifty feet from Chipper's front door. Ben spotted
a mongoose in the dump and started hunting them with
his .22 rifle. Chipper tried counteracting the smell of death
by planting gardenias and tuberoses but the flowers weren't
enough.

"Can't you quit killing mongoose?" I asked Ben.

"I need the practice," he said.

"At least bury the bodies."

"They belong in the dump."

"You're stinking it up for Uncle Chipper."

"I'm not going in there," Ben said, "unless you pay
me."

                    *   *   *

My mother always visited Moloka'i the week before
her trip to Boston. She'd started making summer sojourns
to Bean Town after two women on a Brookline streetcar
convinced her mother Bea they had found money and that
they'd split it three ways. They got Bea off the streetcar,
into their van, and made a grab for her purse. Bea struggled

to find the door handle and fell out of the van—she broke ribs, chipped her pelvis, and fractured her hip. But Bea had held on to her purse. The Flimflam Incident gave my mother an excuse to visit Boston every summer.

Ben and I had beds on the lanai in Gramma's beach house. My mother stayed in the A-frame cottage with my father—she said the peace and quiet made her feel as if her heart might explode. She claimed she needed to get back to Boston to hear the hustle and bustle of an east coast city. "Moloka'i truly is my once-a-year penance," my mother confessed.

The A-frame stood on the site of Gramma's old cottage, the one that had been destroyed by the Tsunami of 1946. It reminded me of a big teepee because of the angle of its roof. Instead of having a cement foundation, it sat on cinder blocks as a precaution against tsunamis and flash floods.

My father had built the A-frame to end my mother's complaints about her lack of privacy. He'd surrounded it with hala trees, bougainvillea, bamboo, and ti plants. It felt as if you were staying at a tropical estate miles from the nearest neighbor. My father knew Gramma liked to spy so he wanted the trees, plants, and flowers to block her view. He claimed the A-frame was a rental but he rarely rented it out. He hated sharing his piece of paradise with anyone, especially during the summers. He also realized Gramma still had bullets left for her antique .219 rifle and he didn't want her firing at tourists whenever she heard a noise or smelled "whiskey on the wind."

Even after the A-frame was built, my mother complained about Hale Kia's "primitive" setting, the noisy geckos, and the lack of "stimulating people and exciting places." She could appreciate the tropics as long as restaurants and boutiques were in striking distance. The east end was torture for her because the only store was Ah Pong's Soda & Sundries, a one-room shanty that had once been a whorehouse. The only outing my mother enjoyed was going to Our Lady of Sorrows Church for Mass. Gramma wasn't allowed to attend the Service because she'd been excommunicated for divorcing Chipper. The women at Our Lady of Sorrows always made a big fuss over my mother, as if they were in the presence of a Hollywood celebrity. She towered over the congregation in her high heels, white gloves, and yellow church hat. Mrs. Friel told my mother she was the spitting image of Carole Lombard. My mother said she was going to Boston to visit Bea.

"The poor woman's recovering from a broken hip," my mother said.

"Auwe," said Mrs. Lima, "good ya go Boston."

                    *   *   *

The summer before my sophomore year, my mother's flight over to Moloka'i coincided with the Kristofersons' arrival by sea. My mother said she was going "stir crazy on Alcatraz" so she invited the Kristofersons over to the A-frame for pupus and drinks. Lisa and Laverne wanted to ride our horses in the afternoon while our parents caught up.

My mother didn't invite Gramma to the pupu party.

She was still seething after my father told her Gramma considered her a part-time wife for abandoning him every summer. "Imagine the nerve of that woman," my mother said.

I picked a green mango for Gramma before the Kristofersons showed up for the party. She peeled it with a paring knife at her koa table—her gnarled fingers guided the blade slowly around the mango. She cut off a slice, dipped it in a bowl of soy sauce, and took a bite.

"Howz it?" I asked.

"Bittah," she said, "but ono."

The phone rang in the kitchen and Gramma got up and answered it. Chipper was on the other end. I sat at the table while Gramma talked. I figured Chipper and Gramma were commiserating since neither one had been invited to the party. "Oh, Chip," Gramma said, "that's terrible." She promised to drive him to Kaunakakai in September. She hung up and returned to the living room.

"Is Uncle Chipper okay?" I asked.

"Can ya keep a secret, Peanut?"

"Yeah."

"Chippa needs an operation."

"For what?"

"Damn fool gotta hernia liftin' a stove."

I heard an engine and looked through the picture frame window. A blue Volkswagen bus puttered past the Norfolk pine and continued along the dirt access road.

"Betta go," Gramma told me.

"I'll stay with you."

"Yoa mutha's expectin' ya."

"Hey, Peanut," Ben called from the lawn, "they're here!"

Leo and Spotty, Gramma's poi dogs, crawled out from beneath the beach house and barked.

"I'll be all right," Gramma told me.

I joined Ben in the coconut grotto between the beach house and the A-frame. He was shooting his Hawaiian sling spear at fallen coconuts. The VW bus pulled off the road and parked beside the A-frame. The side door slid open and the girls jumped out—their long blonde hair shimmered in the sunlight. Lisa and Laverne wore tank tops, jeans, and riding boots. Their kid sister Kathleen had on a yellow sundress. Mr. and Mrs. Kristoferson got out of the bus and followed their girls over to the lounge chairs outside the A-frame. Mr. Kristoferson had on a golf shirt and white shorts. His wife wore a white silk top and capri pants; her hair was cut pixie-style.

My mother sauntered out and greeted everyone in her green dress, pearl earrings, and white sandals. She told the Kristofersons to make themselves comfortable on the lounge chairs. Kathleen sat at the end of her mother's chair holding a Barbie; at ten, she was more interested in playing with dolls than riding horses. My father appeared in his brown polyester shirt and khaki shorts—he joked about being on Hawaiian time and shook hands with Mr. Kristoferson.

"Hui!" Ben called.

Lisa and Laverne spotted us in the grotto and jogged

over. They were seventeen. They'd both modeled for
Liberty House but Laverne quit when the manager told
her to lose a few pounds. Mr. Kristoferson had said Lisa
was his oldest because she was born two minutes and thirty
seconds ahead of Laverne.

Ben fired his spear at a coconut tree and it stuck in
the bark like an arrow. "Wanna ride?" he asked the girls.

"That'd be cool," Lisa said.

"I want Jetty," demanded Laverne.

"Sparkling Eyes is faster," I told her.

Laverne shook her head. "Not with me in the
saddle."

"Laverne's getting ready for the Kentucky Derby,"
Ben teased.

We all walked over to the fence line and slipped
between the wires. Sparkling Eyes and Jetty were already
saddled and tied to the hitching post. Sparkling Eyes was
a young chestnut mare with a white diamond marking on
her forehead. Jetty was fawn-colored and she'd led the
Fourth of July Parade in Kaunakakai. Ben untied the horses
and the girls mounted them and rode off toward the beach.
We'd left the western gate open so they could ride in and
out.

Ben and I walked back to the fence. I heard a
rumble—it was Chipper's old Impala. At first I thought
Chipper was going to Kaunakakai but he turned left at the
Norfolk and eased up the knoll to the beach house. He got
out and toddled to the door while the dogs sniffed the
Impala's tires. Chipper was a tall, lanky man who never

moved fast because he was missing some toes. He wore his visiting clothes: a green and white striped shirt, denims, and a cowboy hat.

"Wonder what he wants?" Ben asked.

"I think he's lonely," I replied.

"That's what he gets for being a drunk."

Ben returned to the coconut grotto while I snuck over to the A-frame and spied through the bamboo. My mother placed monkeypod bowls and a bag of chips on the glass coffee table. The bowls were full of macadamia nuts and clam dunkum. Kathleen sat beside the ti plants playing with Barbie dolls—she placed her Ken doll in front of the Barbie Camper and rolled it over him. My father served drinks and my mother passed around the nuts. My parents pulled up lounge chairs and sat with the Kristofersons.

"That's a good-looking thoroughbred," Mr. Kristoferson said as Lisa trotted along the fringe of ironwoods.

"That's Sparkling Eyes," said my father.

"Your girls are such graceful riders," my mother commented.

"They just adore your beautiful horses," said Mrs. Kristoferson.

My father grabbed a handful of nuts. "Glad somebody does."

All this talk about horses made me feel guilty. Ben and I had our own horses. I had Cody and Ben had Jetty. Both were stocky quarter horses, daughters of Old Sissy. I was always worried that my father would find out I had trouble swinging my saddle from the hitching post onto Cody's back. Ben would saddle for me while our father was roping Sandy, his yellow Arabian. My father had so many rules it took the fun out. He had rules for roping, rules for saddling, and rules for riding. Once I'd failed to secure the belly band because I thought pulling it too tight might hurt Cody—the saddle tilted on Honomuni Beach and I fell. My father circled me on Sandy while Ben rode on ahead to get Cody. "Birdbrain," he said before kicking Sandy in the ribs and galloping off.

Lisa bounced in her saddle as Sparkling Eyes pranced over the lawn. She looked foxy in her red tank top and jeans. She was going to be a senior at Punahou. Lisa liked Ben and me because we always had a horse saddled for her. She looked nothing like Laverne. Laverne was a tomboy with her father's features. Lisa reminded me of Mia Farrow on *Peyton Place*. She could ride either Western or English style. Her versatility impressed me. The girls trotted Sparkling Eyes and Jetty around the coconut grotto and raced through the ironwoods. I ran across the lawn and joined Ben in the grotto.

"Is Lisa our cousin?" I asked him.

"No."

"But isn't she related to Uncle Chipper?"

"Yeah," he said pulling his spear out of a coconut, "but we're not." Ben got tired of spearing and picked up his football. "Yellow, eighteen, blue!"

I pretended to be Jack Snow of the Los Angeles Rams and did a post pattern toward the lounge chairs. The ball hummed through the air and I dropped a bomb in front of Mr. Kristoferson. The ball bounced, rolled, and knocked over the Barbie Camper. Barbie flew out of the driver's seat and landed on the grass.

"Jerk!" Kathleen said.

"Wiener," I replied and retrieved the ball under the A-frame.

"Mom," Kathleen said, "Jeff just called me a wiener!"

"I'm sure he was only fooling," my mother said and sipped her drink. "Weren't you fooling, Jeffrey?"

"Yes," I answered.

Mr. Kristoferson sunk a chip into the clam dunkum. "That Ben's got one hell of an arm."

My father put his drink on the table and squinted at Ben. He pressed his thumb against the bridge of his glasses and pushed them back over his eyes. He stared at Ben as if trying to determine whether Mr. Kristoferson was being sincere.

I stood beside the table, heaved Ben the football, and my pass fell short. Ben retrieved the ball and tossed it straight up. He caught his own pass and tossed another.

"Hope Ben tries out for the Buff 'n' Blue," Mr. Kristoferson said.

"I won't let 'im," said my father.

"Why not?"

"I refuse to sign that release of theirs."

"All the parents sign," Mrs. Kristoferson said, "even the ones with daughters."

My mother scooped dunkum with her chip. "Why,

Louise," my mother said, "what could girls possibly do as dangerous as football?"

"Gymnastics, for one."

"Norm thinks Ben would break his neck playing football."

"He'd break it all right," my father said, "and then I couldn't sue."

Mrs. Kristoferson said her son Tom, who we knew attended a school for bad boys on the Big Island, was the starting fullback for the junior varsity team. She said Tom's muscles were so big they scared her.

"How 'bout a refresher?" my father asked and the Kristofersons passed him their glasses. There was lipstick on my mother's glass but none on Mrs. Kristoferson's. My father returned to the A-frame and my mother talked about her trip to Boston.

"You're gone for the entire summer, Mary?" asked Mrs. Kristoferson.

"Mother is slowing down."

Mr. Kristoferson munched on macadamia nuts. "Didn't she have some trouble back east?"

My mother nodded solemnly. "The poor woman was flimflammed."

Lisa and Laverne returned from their race and trotted through the western gate. Ben and I met them at the saddle room. Sweat glistened on the horses' shoulders and flanks. Ben removed the saddles and the girls helped me with the bridles. I dropped a rope with a slipknot over Sparkling Eyes' head and Ben did the same with Jetty. We led the horses through the pili grass and Laverne swung open the gate to the mauka pasture. Ben and I took the horses in. Cody and Sandy neighed from under a mango tree. Laverne closed the gate and we slipped off the ropes. Sparkling Eyes and Jetty ambled over to the trough and drank the green water.

"That trough's gross," Laverne said.

Lisa looked in and scrunched her nose. "It's polluted."

"Wanna scrub it?" Ben asked.

"You scrub it," Laverne replied.

We talked about Punahou. Laverne said her friend was responsible for the bomb scare that cleared out the classes. Ben claimed Miss Tennyson, his math teacher, was dating an ex-con. Lisa told us the football coach had been arrested for soliciting a prostitute on Hotel Street but President Young didn't fire him because he had a winning season. The girls said this would be their last visit to Moloka'i because next summer they would be getting ready for college on the mainland. Lisa asked if we could get them some pakalolo but Ben said we didn't smoke. Lisa brushed the hair out of her face and flipped it over her ear. It felt as if waves of warm honey were washing over me whenever Lisa spoke. She had small, delicate wrists and the freckles on her arms reminded me of constellations.

Ben punched me in the arm. "Time to hele, Peanut," he said.

We strolled through the pili grass and returned to the A-frame. Mr. Kristoferson stood and stretched when he saw his daughters.

"Aren't you girls going to thank Mr. Gill?" Mrs. Kristoferson asked.

"Thank you, Mr. Gill," Lisa and Laverne said.

"You're very welcome," said my father. "Whenever you girls wanna ride, just gimmee a call."

The Kristofersons thanked my parents for the party and we all meandered over to the VW bus. Mr. Kristoferson slid open the side door and the girls piled in. The fenders were caked with red dirt and their bumper sticker read: "Wouldn't You Rather Be Riding A Mule On Molokai?"

"That's quite a roomy Volkswagen," my mother said.

"Comes in handy with three girls," Mrs. Kristoferson replied climbing into the cab.

Mr. Kristoferson got in and started the engine. "We'll have to take you all out on the *Enchantress*."

"Can we troll?" Ben asked.

"For record marlin," Mr. Kristoferson promised. He backed up and one of his tires crushed a baby coconut.

My parents waved goodbye. Kathleen stuck out her tongue and the girls giggled. Lisa flashed the peace sign through the rear window as the VW putt-putted down the dirt road.

The Impala was still parked in front of the beach house. I felt good about Chipper and Gramma being together. They'd formed a fragile bond that allowed them to deal with loneliness on the ranch and I hoped, given time, the love they once shared would bloom again.

                    *   *   *

Mr. Kristoferson kept his word about going out on the yacht. My mother had already left for Boston but my father told Mr. Kristoferson we'd go. My father informed Ben and me we needed to spruce up our wooden dinghy— he had us paint the oars yellow, polish the oar locks, and inflate the pontoons. Ben and I rolled the dinghy down from its dry dock next to the makai pasture and we anchored it twenty feet offshore. My father studied the owner's manual for his 9.2 outboard and mixed oil and gas in a measuring cup. He pried off the outboard's bonnet and squirted WD-40 on all the parts. He dropped the prop into a steel barrel of water to clear the engine of salt. The engine roared as water bubbled over the barrel.

*   *   *

The day of our excursion on the *Enchantress*, my father clutched the steering arm of the outboard and motored the dinghy through the shallows. Ben was at the bow and I sat in the middle. We all wore T-shirts and swim trunks. My father had said we should wear swim trunks in case we fell overboard in high seas. We entered the harbor and our dinghy struggled against two-foot waves. I looked back at my father—his hair was salt and pepper and blood dotted his chin where he'd cut himself shaving. He kept looking at his watch as if he was late for a business meeting.

We made headway against the waves and closed in on the yacht. It was like a cruise ship compared to our boat. There were portholes in its cabin, a top deck for navigation, and a chrome railing on the bottom deck running stern to bow. It was white with blue trim and it floated on the outer edge of the harbor like a happy whale.

"Now, Ben," my father instructed, "you're in charge of the anchor."

"Aye, aye, Captain Gill," Ben replied.

Water spurted out of the yacht's bilge holes.

"Where's that water coming from?" I asked.

"Their pooper," Ben answered.

My father shook his head. "You boys don't know a god damn thing."

Mr. Kristoferson waved from the top deck. Laverne stood beside him holding the brass wheel—she wore a captain's hat and a white halter top.

"Drop anchor when we get to their stern," my father said.

Ben fingered a link in the anchor's chain. "What's a 'stern?'" he teased.

"Don't be a stupe."

My father idled the outboard and we drifted alongside the *Enchantress*. Its big inboard hummed and the propeller made the water boil. I felt nauseous smelling the exhaust.

"Drop anchor!" my father ordered.

Ben heaved the anchor in.

Mr. Kristoferson threw a thick nylon rope to Ben. Ben held the rope and Mr. Kristoferson pulled us over to a chrome ladder.

"Jeffrey," my father said, "get on board."

"Women and children first," Ben joked.

I grabbed a middle rung, pulled myself over, and climbed up to the deck. Mr. Kristoferson had on shorts, a UCLA muscle tee, and sunglasses. "Welcome aboard!" he said. He was about my father's age but seemed much younger.

Ben climbed the ladder next and joined me on the deck.

My father was last. He climbed the ladder gingerly and kept looking back at the dinghy. He slipped on the deck but Mr. Kristoferson caught and steadied him.

"Louise and Kathleen couldn't make it," Mr. Kristoferson said.

"That's too bad," my father replied.

"Did Lisa come?" I asked.

Mr. Kristoferson smiled. "The princess is sunning herself on the bow."

Poles were mounted on the stern. The footlong lures had resin heads with feather bodies. Mr. Kristoferson told us marlin thought they were flying fish. The hooks were hidden in the feathers and they were twice the size of the hooks we used on our ulua lines. Mr. Kristoferson pressed a button and a winch pulled up the anchor. "Anchors away!" he called to Laverne and we headed south out of the harbor. Maui's Nakalele Point was straight ahead and only six miles away. We powered into the ink blue water. The *Enchantress* handled the five-foot swells easily. In the old days, Gramma had seen a herd of deer swimming for Moloka'i and she figured they'd made the crossing from Maui. It was in these waters my father had speared a hammerhead that attacked Chipper's fish trap. I looked north and saw our dinghy bobbing like a toy.

"Is Laverne steering?" my father asked.

Mr. Kristoferson nodded. "She loves being in charge."

"I hope she knows these waters."

"Laverne's akamai when it comes to the sea."

"Can we troll now?" Ben asked.

"Let's get out a little deeper," Mr. Kristoferson said. "You boys go take a look around." He climbed the ladder to the top deck and my father followed.

Ben and I explored the cabin. The portholes were huge and the one overlooking the stern had been swung open. There was a Formica table with bench seats. A chess board was on the table and pawns were scattered on the carpet. Boxes for Monopoly, Jeopardy, Parcheesi, and Toyland were stacked on a shelf. A photo of Mr. and Mrs. Kristoferson was taped to the wall—a giant blue marlin was hanging off a chain between them.

"Let's go check out Lisa," Ben said.

We headed for the bow. The coastline had faded but I recognized the curve of our bay. I spotted the beach house nestled in the ironwood forest. Hale Kia was green and the clouds looked like snow in the high country.

Lisa was lying near the bow with her arms spread out to catch the sun. Her cotton dress had a print of green, white, and pink hibiscus. Her brown legs stretched over the white deck. A wave struck the bow and water beaded up on her legs.

"Howz it," Ben said.

Lisa opened her eyes. "Hi."

"This yacht's bitchin," he said.

She held out a cellophane package of lemon peel. "Want?"

"Sure," Ben said and took a piece.

She extended the package to me.

I reached in and broke off a hunk. "Thanks, Lisa."

We sat on either side of her and I nibbled on the lemon peel. Lisa told us about her boyfriend Paul Damon. Paul was our starting quarterback and he'd made the ILH All-Star team his junior year. Stanford and Notre Dame had already offered him scholarships. I couldn't believe Lisa had settled for a Jock and suddenly I wanted the Buff 'n' Blue to finish dead last in the ILH. Lisa said Laverne was dating a guy from Kaimuki High.

"Haole?" Ben asked.

"Hawaiian," Lisa whispered. "But don't tell Dad."

"What's wrong with Hawaiian?" I asked.

"Dad only lets us date haoles."

"We're part Hawaiian," Ben told her.

"You don't look it."

"We only have a little," I said.

Lisa nodded. "I see it in your noses."

I felt the bridge of my nose.

"You should go to Kam," Lisa decided.

"Yeah," said Ben, "and get creamed every day after school."

I finished my lemon peel and took another piece. A

wave soaked my shirt so I took it off and knotted it around my waist. The sun felt good against my skin.

"You get used to the waves," Lisa said.

The *Enchantress* turned east and cut the swells at an angle. The splashing stopped and we stretched out next to Lisa. The bow vibrated as we surged forward. I closed my eyes and imagined riding horses. Lisa and I were riding up Hale Kia's mountain because the Russians were bombing Oahu. An atomic bomb fell on Punahou's upper field during a scrimmage and blew the football team to bits. It was up to me and Lisa to start a new civilization.

"Let's troll!" Mr. Kristoferson called.

Ben was on his feet. "Come on, Jeff!"

Lisa kept her eyes closed.

"Aren't you coming, Lisa?" I asked.

"No. I need to work on my tan."

Ben dashed to the stern and I chased after him. Mr. Kristoferson already had one line out. He told Ben to release the line on a second pole and to drop the lure in the water. Ben asked Mr. Kristoferson how far out he wanted it and he said just past the bubbles left by the propeller. My father joined us holding a Bloody Mary.

"Did you see those hooks?" I asked my father.

"Big buggahs," he said swirling his drink.

Mr. Kristoferson gave us the grand tour after the lines were out. He showed us the dining room, the kitchen, and the bunk beds. We went below deck and he pointed out the storage bin beneath the bow that contained an inflatable raft, canned rations, jugs of water, and a flare gun. Ben snatched the flare gun and examined it.

"Put that down," my father said.

"It's okay, Norm," Mr. Kristoferson said, "it's not loaded."

"Is the *Enchantress* made of fiberglass?" Ben asked.

"She sure is. Just like your surfboard."

My father gulped his drink. "Cheesus."

"We don't have surfboards," Ben said.

"Well, anyway," Mr. Kristoferson said, "my yacht's unsinkable."

"Like the *Titanic*," I said.

Mr. Kristoferson took the flare gun away from Ben. "Safer than that."

We returned to the kitchen and Mr. Kristoferson fixed my father another Bloody Mary. He handed me a can of ginger ale and gave Ben two cans. "One for Laverne," he said.

"What about Lisa?" I asked.

"She says soda's bad for her figure."

Ben and I climbed to the top deck. We were a half-mile offshore and heading for Cape Halawa. The cliffs were fuzzy with lantana and ilima bushes. The coastline was rugged and only a few bays were powdered with sand. Ben snuck up behind Laverne and put the cold can against her skin.

"Owie!" Laverne said.

"How's your moke boyfriend?" Ben asked handing her the soda.

Laverne stuck the can in a holder next to the ship's

compass. She kept her eyes straight ahead and both hands on the yacht's wheel.

"Don't worry, Laverne, " Ben said. "We won't tell pops you're hapai."

"Lisa said that?"

Ben laughed. "You'd believe anything."

Ben and Laverne talked about the yacht as the compass shimmied in its glass housing. I stole glances down at Lisa—she'd turned over and the sun struck the backs of her legs. The wind rustled her hair and blew up her dress. She wore pink panties. I winced thinking about Paul Damon pawing her after a game.

"Your dad's a nice man," Laverne said.

"How come?" Ben asked.

"He lets us ride his horses."

"Big deal."

I started feeling sick to my stomach. The ginger ale had mixed with the lemon peel and each rock of the *Enchantress* made me feel worse. I burped to relieve pressure. I told myself it would go away in a few minutes. It didn't. My stomach churned like the propeller. I climbed down the stairs, ran for the stern, and puked into the boiling water.

"Gross!" Ben said.

I turned around and everyone was watching. A sour smell drifted back and Lisa plugged her nose. Mr. Kristoferson shook his head in the cabin. My father finished his Bloody Mary and gnawed on the ice. The pole beside me curved down and the line started grinding off the reel.

Mr. Kristoferson charged out of the cabin—he looked at me and up at Ben. Ben descended slowly and, when he got on the deck, he watched the line shrink on the reel. Finally, Mr. Kristoferson grabbed the pole but the grinding stopped and the line went slack. He tried reeling but there was no tension and the line twisted around itself.

"Blasted fish took my best lure," Mr. Kristoferson groused. "That was my super lucky one."

My father stumbled over. "Musta been a big buggah," he said.

"Musta been a marlin," Ben decided.

Mr. Kristoferson stared at Ben and me. "Too bad no men on board," he said shoving the pole back in its mooring. He climbed the ladder up to Laverne.

"What a time to barf," Ben told me.

I looked toward the bow—Lisa leaned against the railing and gazed across the channel at Maui.

I waited at the stern for the second pole to bend. I prayed for us to land a fish to make the trip good. This was Lisa's last summer on Moloka'i and I wanted her to remember me as the boy who'd landed a marlin. But our luck was gone. I convinced myself I had poisoned the water.

Even when I saw the brilliant arc of flying fish off Mokuhooniki Atoll, I knew I'd ruined everything.

BAD BOYS

Ben got his driver's license at the start of junior year after passing both the written and the road test on his first try. My father said he wished Ben would apply the same hard work and determination when it came to schoolwork. Ben told me it was funny going the speed limit on the road test knowing he'd double it the day he got his license.

Ben took advantage of his license right away. He asked Monica Apianni out and, after they cruised Waikiki in my mother's Barracuda, Ben parked at Lover's Lookout near the Diamond Head lighthouse. After two dates, Monica told Ben she was going back to her old boyfriend from McKinley High. Ben didn't reveal much about what had happened but I thought it had something to do with his inability to say anything meaningful about himself. I'd overheard him on the phone and knew his conversations with the fairer sex were one-sided. He'd ask a barrage of questions that sounded like interrogation and, when it was Ben's turn to talk, he'd respond with simple "yes" or "no" answers and continue on with the third degree.

*   *   *

Ben drove around in the Barracuda after his breakup with Monica. Wayne didn't have his license yet and he loved riding shotgun. Ben said cruising Kalakaua Avenue at night reminded him of the movie *American Graffiti*. He told me he'd gotten the Barracuda up to ninety miles an hour on Diamond Head Road after some locals pulled alongside in a '57 Chevy and the driver stuck his head out and spat at them.

"Twah," Ben said, "twah! That's what it sounded like."

"You mean the Chevy?" I asked.

"No, doofus," he replied, "that's the sound of the Portagee spitting."

"Did you wash the spit off the Barracuda?"

"It flew back and hit the Chevy," he claimed.

*   *   *

It was difficult to discuss girls with Ben. Whenever I tried, he'd clam up. Sometimes he'd crash public school dances in the hopes of finding a local girl who would understand his angst. He made a hasty exit from the Kalani High Dance when a Samoan on crutches threatened to pound him into poi.

I was hardly Don Juan when it came to affairs of the heart. I believed that if love was meant to be it would just happen. A girl in French class named Mindy Birch liked me but I didn't like her because she wore muumuus and seemed conservative. Mindy began wearing tube tops and hip huggers—I got a crush the day I saw her drumming a pen on her tan belly. She agreed to go with me to see *Fritz the Cat*. Even though I only had my learner's permit, I borrowed the Barracuda and drove us to the Queen Theatre in Kaimuki. I put my hand on Mindy's knee during the movie and she brushed it off.

"Don't ask me out again," Mindy said in the dark.

I stopped chewing Milk Duds. "Why not?"

"This movie's antifeminist."

"Hush!" a woman behind us said.

"It's only a cartoon," I whispered.

"You don't know anything, Jeff."

*   *   *

Instead of cracking a book in Study Hall, Ben spent his time rooting through wastebaskets. He found a letter Nina Zappaterra had written asking a girlfriend if she should "give juice" to a student advisor named Hoagie Peabody. Ben made copies and posted them all over campus. Hoagie said, if he ever caught the punk doing the posting, he'd beat him to a pulp. Ben located Hoagie's Fiat in the faculty parking lot and let the air out of his tires.

Dean McQueen spent his mornings pulling down copies of Nina's letter while Ben posted new copies after lunch. During assembly, McQueen said the culprit was a coward. Ben phoned McQueen and told him he was a Nazi. When McQueen asked who was speaking, Ben played a tape of our mother's toilet flushing.

*   *   *

My father said he had something important to discuss with Ben and me a month into our junior year. I figured this was going to be a serious talk because he'd chosen a time when my mother was at her Kahala Women's Guild meeting. He didn't like her around in serious situations because he thought her presence softened the mood. He invited us out on the lanai and he sat on a wicker chair beside the brick wall. Above him was a mosaic of war canoes attacking Easter Island.

"Take a seat, boys," my father said.

"What's this," Ben said, "*Dragnet*?"

"Ha," my father replied.

Ben and I flopped on a new floral couch that was covered with overlapping sheets of plastic. My father had said the couch would last years longer if our skin never touched it. He hated it when Ben or I sat on upholstered furniture without shirts or if we walked on the living room carpet with bare feet. He rarely bought new things for the house because he felt it would only be a matter of time before we destroyed it.

"Well, boys," my father began, "this is your junior year."

"Duh," Ben said.

My father crossed his legs. "I hope you know this year counts."

"For what?" Ben asked.

"For college, naturally. I want you both getting good grades."

Ben shifted his weight on the couch and the plastic beneath him crinkled. "Can I split?"

"No," said my father, "we're discussing your future." He pulled up a fat book and flashed us the cover. "I bought you *The College Handbook*."

"Wow," I said, "there must be jillions of colleges."

My father nodded and opened the book. "If I had my choice," he said fingering the pages, "I'd go to Amherst."

"Why Amherst?" I asked.

He winked at me. "It's surrounded by women's colleges. A guy going to Amherst could get any girl he wanted. Now I'm willing to pay your tuition if you get into a good school."

"Who says I wanna go?" Ben asked.

My father took off his glasses and put one of the stems in his mouth. "What are you planning on doing, Ben? You're certainly not going to sponge off of me."

"I wanna be a racecar driver."

My father chewed on the stem. "Yeah," he said sliding his glasses back on, "and I wanna be President of the United States."

I remembered how intensely Ben had watched TV as Peter Revson took the checkered flag at Laguna Seca. "I think Ben can do it," I said.

"Come on," my father replied. "The odds are a-million-to-one."

Ben yawned. "I didn't say it'd be easy."

"Know what your problem is, Ben?"

"What?"

"You're naive like your mother. Do you honestly think you're going to waltz in and drive the Indy 500? It takes years of training and sacrifice, and that's if you don't die in a crash."

"I won't crash."

"What about your eyes? You've got the worst eyes in the family. Racecar drivers need perfect vision."

"I'll wear my contacts."

My father sat up in his chair. "Look, you god damn fool, you're filling your brain with pipe dreams."

"What's a pipe dream?" I teased.

"Something that never comes true. Your brother thinks just by puttering around Kahala in his mother's car he'll learn how to drive professional tracks at high speeds. If that's not a pipe dream, I don't know what is."

Ben got off the couch and headed back into the house. He walked down the hall and slammed his door.

My father slouched and his face turned ruddy. "What about you, Jeffrey?" he asked. "I hope you wanna go to college."

I nodded. "I'd like to go to Stanford."

"Good boy. Any idea what you'd major in?"

"Well, they gave us this career test at Punahou."

My father sat up. "Oh? What were the results?"

"It said I'd make a great adventurer."

My father shook his head. "Birdbrains," he said, "birdbrains for sons."

*   *   *

Ben took the first step toward becoming a racecar driver when he saw a Lotus Europa for sale in the classifieds. He had two grand saved from working the previous summer for Mahuka Roofing. An Englishman on Tantalus Mountain was selling the Lotus because the cooling system couldn't cope with the combination of his lead foot and the tropical heat—it blew head gaskets left and right. The Englishman had been honest about the car's problems but Ben fell in love with the two-seater after his test drive to the top of Tantalus.

"Mind if I drive to Kahala to show my Dad?" Ben asked.

"Sure," said the Englishman, "but if you wreck it, you buy it."

"I won't wreck it," Ben promised.

I sat in the suicide seat as Ben drove the hairpins down Tantalus and zipped east on the H-1. He took the Waialae Avenue offramp, hung a right after cruising by Kahala Mall, and flew past a Porsche on Aukai Avenue. My father was weeding out front in his lauhala hat and khaki shorts when Ben pulled into the driveway.

Ben climbed out of the Lotus with a big smile. "Like my wheels?"

"Cheesus," my father said. He bent down and tapped the wooden handle of his weeder against the fender. "Is this plastic?"

"Fiberglass," Ben said.

"It's a death trap."

"It's my money."

My father frowned. "You'd be a fool to buy it."

Ben drove the Lotus back to Tantalus and offered two grand. The Englishman coughed and looked at his Asian wife. She smiled and the Englishman shook Ben's hand.

*   *   *

The Lotus looked much more expensive than what Ben had paid for it. Wayne kept asking for rides. Ben drove my mother around Diamond Head Road and she said it made her feel like a movie star. My father refused to get in. Ben was convinced girls would swoon once they saw his wheels. He drove me to school, popped open a compartment between the bucket seats, and pulled out a stiletto with a pearl handle.

"Wow," I said.

He pressed a chrome button on the handle and a blade shot out. "Nobody better monkey."

"Where'd you get it?"

"Dang's Pawn Shop," he said, "on Hotel Street."

Ben pressed the button again and the blade disappeared. He put the stiletto back in the compartment and drove up Palm Drive. He pulled over on the access road next to Old School Hall and dropped me off while Dionne Warwick sang "Walk On By" on his stereo. I shut the door and he burned rubber going the wrong way on a one way outside Dillingham Auditorium. Junior high girls watched him zip around the corner and speed down Palm Drive.

"Who saw me in the Lotus?" Ben quizzed me later.

"These choice chicks."

"What choice chicks?"

"I think they were seventh graders."

"Bummer," he said.

*   *   *

Ben joined the Bad Boys not long after the Lotus blew a head gasket and had to be towed to Waipahu to get fixed. The Bad Boys were a group of aloof haole and Asian seniors who hated everything Punahou stood for, from its image as an elitist school to the fact that all the Hawaiian and Samoan scholarship boys were sweating it out on the football field. The Bad Boys congregated outside McNeil Auditorium and leaned against the white stucco wall. The Vietnam War was winding down and they taunted boys walking by in ROTC uniforms. Ben had dropped out of ROTC because he hated all the drills and marching. When the mayor paraded through campus to deliver a speech, Ben hurled a rotten mango that splattered his suit. Dean McQueen questioned the Bad Boys but they denied any involvement.

"I saw you with those seniors," I told Ben.

"Don't come around," he said.

"Why not?"

"I don't want 'em knowing we're related."

"What's the big deal, Juicy?"

"You're a dork."

McNeil Auditorium was perfect for the Bad Boys because it stood apart from the rest of campus—from there you could see the Brains playing chess outside Bingham

Hall, the Jocks shooting the bull on the benches in front of Cooke Library, the Party Girls gossiping under the monkeypod trees, and the Surfers reenacting rides on the steps of Old School Hall. From that vantage, fellow students were reduced to the size of bugs. The Bad Boys amused themselves by smoking and using felt pens to doodle on the wall, doodles that expanded into a universe of geometric shapes, local sayings, and antiestablishment cartoons. Ben added crucified likenesses of Dean McQueen and President Young. A reporter from *Ka Punahou* said they were creating pop art and a photo appeared on the front page. The next morning, Mr. Tanaka and his fastidious crew used brushes and cleanser to vaporize everything the Bad Boys had created.

THE DRUG CLUB

Senior year arrived and it felt like I was standing on the edge of a cliff without a parachute. I sensed that underclassmen were looking up to seniors to set an example but I didn't know what kind of example to set. It was as if, once you made it to your final year, everyone expected you to set the world on fire. I'd barely gotten my driver's license after flunking my first road test for speeding and I'd just managed to scrape together five hundred dollars to buy an orange Datsun B-210 with bald tires, a coat hanger for an antennae, and a temperamental carburetor. I was also faced with the pressure of taking the SAT and completing college aps. I'd requested and received an application from Stanford University only to discover that, besides having to write a personal essay saying how you'd give your eye teeth to attend their precious institution, you had to produce letters of recommendation as well as fill in all the empty spaces with lists of political exploits, athletic awards, scholastic prizes, and extraordinary feats. I couldn't think of a single thing to put down. Should I say that I was vice president of the carnival's Haunted House Committee? That sounded lame. What about captain of the winning basketball team in the PE tourney? No. I was mad at myself for not doing better in school and for not trying to at least fake an extracurricular existence by joining a few boring clubs or making a team that made you exercise your guts out after school. I did try out for the track team but the coach was more interested in furthering his streak of consecutive state titles than inspiring a fledgling runner.

"Put down that you were in the Boy Scouts," my mother suggested.

"They want the high school years," I said leafing through the application.

"Oh," she replied. "What about that time you helped me sell Cokes at Diamond Head Community Theatre?"

"Yeah," I nodded, "and what about all those Sundays I went with you to Mass?"

"Well, Stanford should know you're a good Catholic."

I laughed. "Wow, Mom, that'll put me at the top of the heap, above the guy with the A-plus average who's also class president and the girl who discovered the cure for polio."

"My, which girl was that?"

"I was just kidding, Mom."

"You used to be a nice boy," she replied.

*   *   *

I did have extracurricular activities at Punahou, only they weren't meant for college applications. One of those activities included accompanying my friend Steve Johnson on his drug deals. We'd go off-campus and hang out outside the Lutheran Church—that's where Steve sold his magic mushrooms, Maui Wowie, Bangkok hash, and hash oil. The hash was being smuggled into Hawaii in hollowed-out surfboards and Steve knew the smuggler's brother so he got a good deal. He'd carry his drugs and paraphernalia, including a scale he'd ripped off from chemistry lab, in a fluorescent green cosmetic case that had once belonged to his mother. Steve's green case was a beacon to students searching for mind-altering substances. Everyone from the Jocks to the Brains showed up on the church lawn. Even ROTC cadets marched across the street. Drugs had a way of bringing people together.

Steve had done our lighting in the Haunted House but we hadn't become friends until his chemistry textbook was stolen and I let him borrow mine on weekends. He'd been a Brain until his father died flying helicopter missions into Cambodia. He'd always thought of his father as a hero and, with him gone, he lost his desire to do well in school. He didn't look like a typical Druggie because he kept his blond hair short and wore glasses with lenses as thick as Coke bottles. Steve claimed the combination of hash and blotter acid had damaged his eyesight. He couldn't wear contacts because his corneas were warped. Steve said drugs were destroying his sense of sight but they made up for it by stimulating his mind. Because most of the money he made supported his consumption of hash oil, he only ate two scoops of rice and gravy for lunch and quit buying new clothes. He shopped at Big 88 Surplus in Makiki. Steve was the first to wear camouflage pants to school and he started a craze that swept through campus. Dean McQueen said it was a slam against the military. A foxy teacher named Miss Meyer made a camouflage skirt. It didn't take long for Sears and Liberty House to catch on and create entire camouflage sections. When I told Steve he should get a percentage, he said he'd gladly sell his rights for a quart of hash oil.

*   *   *

The closest I'd come to getting high was raising Kona Gold in plastic buckets out in the backyard. I'd planted seeds in the high potency mix my father used for his hydrangeas and they germinated in three days. Because the breadfruit and hala trees shaded the low areas, I put the buckets on the shake roof to catch more sun. They were a foot tall in a month and my father never noticed. Steve asked to see the plants one day after school—he claimed he had visitation rights since he'd provided the seeds. He followed me in his Dodge Dart and parked behind my orange B-210 out in the driveway. We snuck through the back gate. Steve and I stood on patio chairs and we took six buckets off the edge of the roof.

"Primo leaf," Steve said. He examined each plant as if he was a doctor making a house call—he sniffed shoots, squeezed stalks, and cut leaves with a Swiss Army knife attached to his key chain. I could see my mother through the screen door preparing dinner. Steve started pinching the shoots. "This'll help production," he said.

I was nervous because it was almost pau hana time and my father would be pulling into the driveway. "Can we speed things up?" I asked.

"Mellow out," he replied.

My mother slid open the screen door and strolled across the lanai carrying a bowl full of raw hamburger, bread crumbs, and eggs. She was making meat loaf using a recipe her Aunt Priscilla had sent her from *The Boston Globe*. My mother considered anything that came from that paper as important as the Word of God. "Hello, Steve," she said kneading the ingredients with one hand.

Steve continued pinching. "Howz it, Mrs. Gill."

"Would you boys like a cold drink?"

"No, Mom."

"Could use a beer," Steve said.

"How about some nice guava juice?"

"Beer's got more vitamins," Steve replied.

My mother walked out to the lawn. "My," she said, "what beautiful plants. Is that really marijuana?"

Steve pulled a joint from the pocket of his Aloha shirt. "Wanna toke?"

"Oh, no," my mother said. "I don't want to take a bad trip."

"You only get that from LSD," I said.

"You boys aren't taking LSD, are you?"

"Only when I surf," Steve replied.

My mother massaged the bread crumbs and eggs

into the hamburger. "Better hide those plants," she said, "before you-know-who gets home."

*   *   *

My plants were three feet tall in no time. The females were sending out glistening white hairs and the tips of some of the hairs were turning red. The plants smelled sweet and wild. Two were males and I was tempted to pull them up by the roots because they could fertilize the females and turn the buds to seed. Instead of destroying them, I clipped off their pollen balls.

*   *   *

Akino, our cleaning lady, was sweeping the lanai while I filled a pitcher at the outdoor faucet. She was a short woman with a good sense of humor. Akino had been a picture bride who came to the islands to marry a Japanese man who paid for her passage from Tokyo. Now she was a grandmother. Akino rested the broom against the trunk of the breadfruit tree and looked up at the roof. "What kine plant dat?" she asked.

I unscrewed the cap on a bottle of Gaviota Orchid Bloom and poured some into the pitcher. "Poinsettias."

"I neva see poinsettia like dat."

I pulled a chair over, stood on it, and watered the plants. "They're a special breed," I said, "from Kona."

Akino grabbed the broom and continued sweeping. "Ya get da green thumb," she told me, "just like yoa faddah."

*   *   *

Before I'd made a dime selling pakalolo, Ben

demanded twenty-five percent of my profits as hush money.
I offered fifteen percent. He refused and tortured me with
stories of HPD helicopters flying by with infra red sensors.
He said the fuzz could spot pakalolo on rooftops.

"They're getting your cell ready," Ben said, "at Oahu
State Prison."

"You're lying about those sensors."

"Jailbird."

Steve showed me an article about drug busts in *High
Times*. The sensors really did exist. "Airborne narcs," Steve
warned. Whenever I heard a chopper, I'd run out, pull the
plants off the roof, and hide them in my room.
Lawnmowers, chainsaws, and motorcycles started
sounding like helicopters. Ben said Five-O was closing in
and that I'd have a Samoan boyfriend in prison. The plants
stared dropping leaves because of the constant shifts in
location. Bud production waned. I phoned Steve and he
took the plants away.

*   *   *

Steve scheduled his drug deals when Church wasn't
in session. He didn't like the idea of ministers lecturing
and people praying while he made illegal transactions fifty
feet away. There was a cemetery and Steve said a ghost
might haunt him if he sold drugs during Service. We got
there early one day and waited under a coconut tree for
the noon Service to end. Steve rolled gram weights around
in his hand as if they were marbles or ball bearings—he
reminded me of the pupule captain portrayed by
Humphrey Bogart in *The Caine Mutiny*. Parishioners began

filing out and Steve flipped open his green case. He pulled out a scalpel and a sharpening stone. An Asian woman picked her way past us with a cane. Steve wiped the blade off on his camouflage pants and rubbed one side against the stone. A breeze came up and the fronds on the coconut tree rustled. Steve turned the blade over and sharpened the other side. He tested its edge by pressing it against his thumb and shaving off a piece of skin. He pulled out a block of black hash and rested it on the stone. The hash had a pungent odor.

"Smells like kukae," I said.

"It's not kukae." He began slicing off squares as if it was a block of butter.

I looked across Punahou Street and saw Hoagie, our student advisor on loan from Princeton University. President Young thought Hoagie was a great role model because he attended an Ivy League school. Hoagie waited for traffic to ease. A car stopped and he jogged across the street.

"Narc," I said.

Steve looked up from his work. "Client."

"Come on," I said, "that's McQueen's fink."

"Hoagie boy's my one o'clock."

Hoagie jumped the curb as if it was a hurdle and sauntered toward us. There was something cocky about the way he swung his arms. "That looks sweet enough to eat," Hoagie said squatting down next to Steve.

"The usual?" Steve asked.

"Double," Hoagie replied. His hair was dark brown

and he had sideburns like the singer Tom Jones. A red pencil was tucked behind his ear. He wore a long sleeve shirt, pleated slacks, and flip-flops. Rumor had it that Hoagie had already nailed three cheerleaders and was working on the girls in the Pep Club. Most of the girls and even some of the women teachers swooned whenever he walked by. I considered Hoagie a poacher. His age and status gave him an unfair advantage. I figured the main reason he'd picked Punahou was because of our girls. He'd dated Dawn Yamashita his first week on campus and Dawn cried her eyes out during a movie McQueen made the seniors watch. In the movie, this naive girl is seduced by a jerk and there are all these corny allusions to sex, like a jackhammer busting through asphalt and a pile driver pounding a pile through the ground. Wayne said, "Geev um, Hoagie!" and everyone laughed. Dawn ran sobbing out of McNeil Auditorium.

Ben had heard that Hoagie would start out by advising a girl and then invite her over to his studio to see his Princeton yearbook—it wouldn't be long before he had her on his waterbed.

"How's the sex life, Hoagie?" Steve asked.

Hoagie frowned. "These Punahou chicks make you work."

"Thought you scored Nina Zappaterra?"

"Skin-on-skin," he said. He rolled over on his belly and did pushups on the lawn. The red pencil didn't fall out as he went up and down. It was as if the pencil was glued to his head. "It's tough getting the juice."

"What about Princeton?" I asked.

"What about it?"

"Don't you get any juice over there?"

"Gallons," Hoagie said. He quit doing pushups, rolled over next to us, and stared up at the sky. "Who you studs dating?"

I shook my head. "No one."

Steve pulled the scale out of his green case. He whistled to the tune of "Born to be Wild" and set up the scale on a flat patch of grass. He placed gram weights on one side and a square of hash on the other. "There's this chick at Kalani," Steve told Hoagie.

"With all this choice meat running around at Punahou?"

"I've been to Hotel Street," I lied.

Hoagie sat up. "Smart man," he said sliding the pencil out from behind his ear. He used the pencil to dig dirt out from beneath his big toenail.

"Hey, Hoagie," I said, "does Princeton take C-plus students?"

Hoagie started in on the other big toe. "Are you Punahou's starting quarterback?"

"Once I tried out for the track team."

"Tried out? Didn't you make it?"

"No."

Hoagie shook his head. "Are you student body president?"

"I hate politics."

Hoagie slid the pencil back behind his ear and

watched Steve try to balance the hash against two grams. The scale tipped in favor of the hash and Steve shaved off a sliver with his scalpel.

"How 'bout clubs?" Hoagie asked me. "Organizations?"

"All Jeff does is watch me deal," Steve said.

"The Drug Club," Hoagie said. "Got any Hawaiian blood?"

"One-sixteenth."

The scale balanced. Steve plucked the hash off the scale and wrapped it in foil. "Jeff's a minor minority," he said.

"Will any college take me?" I asked.

Hoagie locked his hands behind his head and stretched. "There is one," he said, "but that's only 'cause they score outta state tuition."

"Which one?"

"If I get a treat," Hoagie said, "I'll tell."

"No treats," Steve said, "store policy."

"Remember those plants I gave you?" I reminded him.

"Pakalolo?" asked Hoagie.

Steve grimaced. He rooted through the vials and baggies in his case. He pulled out a baggie and examined its contents. "I'll throw in a 'shroom."

Hoagie looked up at the steeple. "Two 'shrooms."

Steve nodded. "That's still forty."

"Sure they're magic?" Hoagie asked reaching for his wallet.

"Picked 'em myself in Mokuleia."

"They'll give you illusions," I said.

Steve dropped the foil-wrapped hash and the mushrooms into a plastic baggie while Hoagie counted out tens and fives and stacked them on one side of the scale. Steve grabbed the money, passed Hoagie the baggie, and wedged the scale back in the case. "Mahalo for shopping at Steve's," he said and shut the lid.

Hoagie slipped the baggie into his shirt pocket and stood up. "Gotta hele," he said. "Nina's waiting at the snack shop."

"What about that college?" I asked him.

"What college?"

"The one you said might take me."

"Try the University of Colorado," he said, "at Boulder."

"Mahalo," I replied. "Hey, Hoagie, do they do drugs at Princeton?"

"Everyone I know drops acid before their morning classes."

"Far-out," said Steve.

Hoagie patted the baggie through his shirt pocket and looked down at me suspiciously. "Hey, man," he said, "are you a narc or something?"

"No," I replied.

Hoagie crossed Punahou Street against heavy traffic and disappeared behind a wall of night-blooming cereus. I was certain he would lead a life impervious to injury no matter how close he came to danger. He was the kind of guy who knew the way to act and the things to say to get what he wanted.

Steve pulled out a vial of hash oil and heated the bottom of the vial with his Bic lighter. The oil began to smoke. He sucked the smoke into his lungs through a glass straw. "Want?" he asked offering me the vial.

I shook my head. While Steve inhaled, I prayed Nina would never give Hoagie the juice.

THE FIGHT OF THE CENTURY

I studied everything from art history to oceanography in my senior year. It didn't hurt that Miss Meyer, my art history teacher, was the foxiest woman on campus or that oceanography meant taking field trips with girls in bikinis. I continued shooting hoops in the driveway and fantasized about playing for the New York Knicks. I met a boxing promoter named Big Nose Espinda at Kaimuki Gas & Go who told me, through rigorous training and sacrifice, I might become the next heavyweight champ of Honolulu.

"But I only weigh one-sixty," I said.

"How big yoa faddah?"

"One-ninety."

"Ya grow."

I told him my last name was Gill and that my Great Uncle Sharkey had trained Bobo Olson.

"Shoulda told me dat right off da bat," Big Nose said.

"Sharkey stay trainin' my Tongan ova Kalihi side. Go check dem out."

"I don't wanna get in Sharkey's way."

Big Nose climbed into his Caddy. "No pilikia," he said, "maybe one day, ya fight foa me."

*   *   *

I drove my B-210 to Kalihi and parked on a dirt driveway near Farrington High. I pushed open the gym's double doors—a Tongan was in the ring sparring with a bald haole. The Tongan had the haole pinned against the ropes and he hooked him hard to the body.

Heavy bags hung off chains near the entrance to the locker room. The bags were patched with duct tape. Speed bag platforms were mounted on opposite sides of the gym. Fight posters covered the walls—Rocky Marciano vs. Joe Louis, Floyd Patterson vs. Ingemar Johansson, and Cassius Clay vs. Sonny Liston. A poster for Sugar Ray Robinson vs. Bobo Olson was framed. Gramma had said her brother Sharkey discovered Bobo when Bobo was a boy running through traffic on Bishop Street selling newspapers.

Bleachers were set up beside the ring but the only spectator was a Filipino man with a Honolulu Islanders baseball cap pulled down over his eyes. I walked by and heard him snoring. A black fighter walked out of the locker room and began bobbing and weaving around a heavy bag. His blows sounded like gunshots.

A wiry man with a hat jogged out of the locker room. He headed for the ring and leaned over the top rope. I knew from pictures he was Sharkey, Gramma's younger brother. I'd never met him. He wore white slacks, a maroon jacket, and a fedora. He held a stopwatch in one hand and a roll of gauze in the other. His fedora had a peacock feather with an iridescent eye. That eye seemed to watch me as I walked on a floor of blue mats splattered with bird droppings. I looked up—doves roosted in the rafters. Open windows high on the walls allowed birds to fly in and out.

Gramma had told me that a gang called "the Barefoot Boys" ruled Waikiki Beach during the Roarin' Twenties. Malahinis at the Moana and the Royal Hawaiian paid them for surf lessons and outrigger canoe rides. Gramma said the Barefoot Boys beat up her brother Tommy when they caught him kissing one of their girlfriends. Sharkey had just started managing Purple, a piha kanaka maoli heavyweight from Papakolea with skin so dark it glowed. Gramma told Sharkey about Tommy's beating and he hiked into the hills of Papakolea to find Purple while his younger brother Jackie went downtown. Jackie whistled on Hotel Street—old timers who'd trained with Jackie at CYO Gym stuck their heads out of pool halls and roominghouse windows. The word went out that the Gill brothers needed help. Jackie and the old time boxers met up with Sharkey and Purple in Kapahulu and they all went down to Waikiki. Gramma was teaching my father how to swim when she saw Purple tip over a lifeguard tower in front of the Moana. Duke Kahanamoku surfed in and told Sharkey to quit making pilikia. Sharkey told Duke this was family business. Duke looked toward Diamond Head and saw thirty Barefoot Boys heading toward them. They all wore red

swim trunks and had black footprint tattoos on their
shoulders. Their leader was Babooze, a huge Puerto Rican
wearing brass knuckles.

Duke dropped his surfboard in the water. "Ya get
moah guts dan brains, Sharkbait," he said and paddled back
out.

The Barefoot Boys surrounded Sharkey's boxers.

"Dis our beach," Babooze said.

"Who says?" asked Purple.

Babooze laughed. "I says."

Two squad cars showed up and parked on Kalakaua
Avenue. The police officers got out and watched from the
boardwalk.

"Yoa boys wen' jump my big bruddah," Sharkey told
Babooze.

Babooze spit in the sand. "Yoa bruddah got whacha
gettin'."

"What I gettin'?"

"One good kine whippin'," Babooze said and he hit
Purple in the mouth with the brass knuckles—Purple's front
teeth flew out and the fight was on. Sharkey pounded one
Barefoot Boy with lightning jabs. A second had a knife and,
when he missed Sharkey on his first lunge, Jackie sent him
flying with a right cross. A Barefoot Boy hit an old timer
and slammed his face against the hull of an outrigger canoe.
A Filipino boxer decked a Barefoot Boy with an uppercut.
Babooze hammered away at Purple with his brass knuckles.
A Hawaiian boy threw a coconut and hit Babooze in the
head. Babooze chased the boy and Jackie tripped Babooze.

Babooze got up and Purple threw a roundhouse that opened a gash on the Puerto Rican's forehead. Babooze started throwing wild. A Barefoot Boy swung a paddle at a Japanese boxer—the boxer ducked and countered with a straight left that sent the Barefoot Boy reeling. Purple picked up a redwood surfboard and slammed in down on Babooze's head. Babooze was groggy. Purple went on the attack, hitting the big Puerto Rican with vicious hooks and uppercuts.

"Break his hat!" Sharkey said.

Purple delivered a straight right to the jaw and Babooze fell. The Barefoot Boys ran for their lives. Purple dragged Babooze by the heels down to the surf and held his head under the waves.

Sharkey waded out and tapped Purple on the shoulder. "I t'ink dat buggah wen' learn his lesson."

They carried the choking Babooze back to shore and left him next to the overturned lifeguard tower. The police drove off without arresting anyone.

I walked around the ring to get a closer look at Sharkey. His arms seemed translucent—veins swirled around inside him like blue piping. "Ova-hand, foa chrissakes," he said. He got his name after being called "Sharkbait" as a boy. He was tall and thin but his forearms bulged with muscle. A pair of bulbous ears made his fedora sit high on his head. His expression said he'd seen it all and nothing you could do or say would surprise him.

"Hi, Uncle Sharkey," I said.

"Kulikuli," he said watching his fighters. "Bus' um

up, Tiny. Break dat haole's hat."

"Uncle Sharkey?"

He looked down. "Whacha want?"

"Big Nose sent me."

"Dat buggah owes me kala."

"I'm Jeffrey. Norman Gill's son."

Sharkey frowned. "No look like one Gill," he said.
Sharkey spoke a creole similar to Gramma's but you'd never
know they were brother and sister. Decades of boxing and
barroom brawls had taken their toll—his nose was bent,
his cheekbones flattened, and his ears cauliflowered.
Networks of tiny red veins on his cheeks looked like spider
webs. "What school ya go?" he asked me.

"Punahou."

"Watch Tiny's feet," Sharkey said. "See how dey
move?"

I turned my attention to the boxers. "Who's Tiny?"

"Da damn tiny talofa, who'd ya think?"

"Who's the haole?"

"Mistah Clean."

Tiny got trapped along the ropes. He whacked Mr.
Clean's head with a left hook and backed him into a corner
with a series of jabs. Mr. Clean threw a wild right. Tiny
crouched down and connected with an uppercut that sent
Mr. Clean reeling into the turnbuckle.

"Ya cookin' wit' gas, Tiny," Sharkey said. "Now
double up."

Tiny threw a pair of hooks that smacked Mr. Clean's
head. Mr. Clean went down to one knee and put a glove to

his face. Drops of blood hit the canvas from a cut above his eye.

Sharkey checked his stopwatch. "Pau hana."

Tiny and Mr. Clean tapped gloves. Tiny picked up a bottle of water and they passed it between their gloved hands.

"Fuckin' laced me," Mr. Clean told Tiny.

Tiny took a swig. "Moah betta hele on to Hollywood, brah."

"With a face like hamburger?" Mr. Clean asked climbing out of the ring.

"Lemmee see dat eye," Sharkey said and Mr. Clean stumbled over. Sharkey wiped off the blood with a towel and applied Vaseline with a Q-tip to the cut.

Mr. Clean grimaced. "That stings, man."

"Quit ya yelpin'," Sharkey said taking off Mr. Clean's gloves, "dat's no biggah dan a flea bite."

Tiny slipped through the ropes, walked over to a padded bench, and rolled over on his belly. He did pushups on the bench with his gloves on.

"Tiny's a madman," Mr. Clean told Sharkey.

"Whacha expect from one Tongan?" Sharkey asked. "No fightin' foa one week."

"I still get the forty?"

"Ya get it. Now hit da showah."

"Who's the kid?" Mr. Clean asked nodding at me.

"Some puhi'u says I'm his uncle."

"Hey, kid," Mr. Clean said, "want some advice?"

"Sure."

"Stay away from this game," he said and shadow-boxed his way back to the locker room.

Sharkey picked up a medicine ball and headed over to the bench. He held the ball over Tiny's back. "Roll ova."

Tiny rolled over and Sharkey slammed the ball down on his belly, again and again. Tiny grunted after each slam.

"Get breadfruit in dat gut?" Sharkey asked him.

"Squid."

"Eat fish an' poi."

Tiny rolled onto his belly and Sharkey karate-chopped his shoulders. A dove flew down from the rafters and landed on the turnbuckle—it pecked at the top rope.

"What should I do?" I asked.

Sharkey stopped chopping and looked me over, head to toe. "Shadowbox da mirrah."

A narrow, full-length mirror was mounted on the wall.

"Show me whacha got, Punahou," Sharkey said.

"But there's no shadow to box."

"Kulikuli an' t'row."

I took a boxer's stance in front of the mirror. I felt foolish in my PE shorts, white tee, and sneakers. I threw out a slow right followed by an even slower left. I repeated the punches and it felt as if I was moving in slow motion. My blows lacked power and I looked over at Sharkey for help.

"Flat foot floogies," he said.

I tried dancing on the balls of my feet but I felt awkward. I stopped throwing and just stood there with my hands up.

"Punahou keeds stay soft," Sharkey said, "good-foa-nut'in'."

"Moelepo," I said.

"Dat's right."

I crouched, threw a left, and followed that up with a hook. I pretended Wayne was charging through the mirror and I hit him with a right lead. Wayne countered with a left jab but I slipped his punch and connected with a left hook to the jaw. He hit me with an overhand right but missed with a left uppercut. I backed up and tripped on the mat.

"Quit playin'," Sharkey told me.

"I'm not playing."

"Yeah, yeah, yeah."

Tiny returned to the ring and stood in one corner with his gloves down.

"Three rounds hard," Sharkey told Tiny.

Tiny started jabbing. He was right-handed because he led with his left and followed with his right. His punches were short and crisp and he threw them in combinations. He backed an imaginary opponent up into a corner and turned to fight out of the same corner. He drove his opponent into the middle of the ring with uppercuts. He had a look of determination that said he'd take five punches just to land one good shot. He was a slugger who liked to go to the body. He kept his hands up and his elbows in to protect his ribs.

I picked up a bottle of water and took a gulp.

Someone poked me in the back. "No suck da waddah."

I turned around—it was the Filipino man with the baseball cap.

"Chy sip," he suggested. "Too much waddah no good." He motioned for the jug and I handed it too him. He took a sip, gargled, and swallowed. "Ono," he said. He sipped again, spit the water out, and returned to the bleachers.

"Dat's Alfredo Hadulco," Sharkey called out to me. "Lightweight Champ of Hanalulu, afta da big war."

I looked over at the bleachers. Alfredo sat with the visor of his cap pulled down over his eyes.

"Had one crook foa managa," Sharkey said, "stole da buggah blind."

"What's Alfredo do now?"

"Talk story," Sharkey said. "Get back to dat mirrah, Punahou."

I returned to the mirror and Sharkey stood behind me. He snapped out a straight left jab and a straight right. "Taught yoa ol' man how to box," he said, "den he wen' kick dis big Portagee's ass."

"He did?"

"Geev um dirty lickins ova at Saint Louis."

"My father said you put him through hell." I don't know why I said it but it just rolled off my tongue.

"He said dat?"

"Yeah."

"Whateva t'ings yoa faddah says I did," Sharkey

replied, "I did 'em ten times worse."

"Teach me what you taught him."

"No can," Sharkey said. "Ya stay one southpaw. Gotta teach ya different. Who da punk ya wanna beef?"

"Nobody."

"Must be one punk. Odahwise, ya wouldn't be heah."

I put up my fists and held my elbows against my ribs. "Wayne Braswell," I said, "captain of the volleyball team."

"Dat one wahine sport."

"Maybe in the old days."

"Haole boy?"

I nodded. "He's a royal prick."

"Eh! Watch yoa language in my gym."

"Sorry."

"Big buggah?"

"Forty pounds heavier, five inches taller."

"Da biggah dey stay," Sharkey said, "da harda dey fall." Sharkey nudged me aside and stared at his reflection. He threw out a succession of long straight jabs with both hands and developed a rocking motion by shifting his weight from one foot to the other. The jabs got faster and faster and Sharkey made a whistling noise through his nose. "Teach ya to break his hat," he said.

Gramma had said Sharkey fought outlaw fights when Hawaii was a Territory and boxing was illegal. The fights had no refs, no weigh-ins, and no gloves. There wasn't even a ring—just an agreement to meet at Kapiolani

Park. The winner got one hundred dollars in gold. Despite attempts to keep the fights a secret, thousands of spectators showed up. Odds were posted on a coconut tree and bets were made. Spectators closest to the boxers formed a human ring. "Fought 'til one of um dropped," Gramma'd said. Sharkey was so badly beaten once by an Australian fighter he went blind for a week. His sight came back and he returned to Kapiolani Park for a rematch—he knocked the Australian out in the second round.

"Step into da punches," Sharkey told me, "snap dem out, bring dem back in."

I stood in front of the mirror and snapped out a right and a left in succession.

"T'ink of dem as springs," Sharkey said.

I threw combinations and Sharkey shook his head. "Droppin' yoa hands, Punahou, showin' yoa ribs." He pulled out a roll of gauze from the side pocket of his jacket and anchored the end around the thumb of my right hand. He crisscrossed gauze over the top of my hand and in-between the fingers. "Small kine wrists," he said. "Ya muddah from wheah?"

"Boston."

"No wonda. Ya get east coast wrists."

"What's wrong with east coast wrists?"

"Easy to busticate," he said. "Get in da ring."

"You mean, fight?"

"Tiny show ya da ropes," he said wrapping my left hand. "Ya wanna learn, don't ya?"

"Not in one day."

"Trial by fiah. Sink or swim."

"I should train first, Uncle Sharkey."

"Ya 'mind me of yoa faddah." He pulled two squares of foam padding out of his jacket pocket. "Dis da secret," he whispered.

"What secret?"

"Da foam." He placed the foam squares on my padded knuckles and used tape to secure them. He pulled red Everlast gloves over my hands and cinched them up. "Listen," he whispered, "ya pound dis talofa. No scared um."

"Isn't he a pro?"

"Open ya yap."

I opened my mouth and he shoved in a chunk of green rubber from a garden hose.

"Bite down," he said.

I clamped down on the rubber and slipped between the top and middle ropes. Tiny shadowboxed in his corner. The canvas floor was springy and I danced around to get the feel of the ring. Sharkey had put each of his three sons in the ring upon turning sixteen. Each son had gotten the living daylights knocked out of him by a pro. Sharkey had wanted to discourage them from pursuing careers as boxers because he feared they might get hurt or even killed in the ring. I wondered if Sharkey had that same plan in store for me. I bounced around and told myself that, even if Tiny destroyed me, I'd land one good punch.

"Beef!" Sharkey said.

Tiny met me in the middle of the ring. He circled to

my right and moved away from my left. He led with a left hook and pulled it so that it tapped me on the cheek and followed that up with a right that patted my chest. I threw a lazy right and Tiny backpedaled into the ropes.

"What's dis malarkey?" Sharkey asked. "Mix it up."

Tiny jabbed at my face and slapped my belly with an open glove. I side-stepped his jabs and moved to his right. He plodded along and I knew he was taking it easy. I flicked out a couple of rights that he brushed away with his glove. He smiled through his blue mouthpiece and threw a lead right. The punch hit my cheek and sent me into the ropes. I bounced off the ropes and he hit me again, this time with a left hook to the head.

Sharkey karate-chopped the top rope. "Droppin' ya hands, Punahou."

I held up my hands and my arms felt heavy.

"Glass jaw," Sharkey said.

I looked over at Sharkey and that's when Tiny launched a lead right that hit me in the jaw with such force that the chunk of rubber flew out of my mouth. Sharkey went into hysterics. I got mad and went after Tiny, swinging with both hands.

"T'rowin' wild, Punahou!"

Tiny punched my left arm and the blow paralyzed it. He did the same to my right and I dodged an uppercut. He pinned me up against the ropes, faked a left to my head, and delivered a slapping hook to my belly.

"Hit dat talofa," Sharkey said.

Tiny spit out his mouthpiece and glared at Sharkey.

"Fuckin' Sharkbait."

"What?" Sharkey asked Tiny. "No can take one joke?"

"I doin' ya one favah wit' dis kid."

"Yeah, yeah, yeah," Sharkey said. "Get outta da ring, Punahou."

I climbed out and Sharkey took off my gloves. My hands shook. "How come they're shaking?" I asked.

Sharkey removed the tape and foam. "East coast wrists."

Tiny placed his gloved hands over the turnbuckle and stretched.

"Buy gloves," Sharkey said unwinding the gauze, "spar with yoa bruddah. How old is he now?"

"Ben's eighteen," I said.

"Just miss Vietnam."

"I doubt he'd have gone."

"Yoa faddah did."

"That was a different war."

"War is war," Sharkey said.

Tiny climbed out of the ring and lifted a jug of water with his gloved hands. He sipped and spit water out on the mat. He jogged over to the heavy bag and unloaded a barrage of hooks and uppercuts. He liked hitting the bag where it was duct-taped.

"Ya need one fightin' name," Sharkey told me.

"I can't think of anything."

Tiny shadowboxed his way over. "Like 'Killa Kawalski,' " he said while dodging and feigning, "or

'Wildman George.' "

"The Rainbow Warrior," I said.

"Gotta soun' mean," Sharkey said.

"Sound mean to me," said Tiny as he crouched and threw a perfect uppercut.

*   *   *

The Tiny Tongan knocked out a Chicago fighter in the third round of their middleweight fight at the HIC. It was a huge upset and the crowd went pupule. It took a ringside doctor five minutes to revive Tiny's opponent.

The day after Tiny's fight, I returned to the gym feeling more confident. A black boxer Sharkey called "Da Battlah" skipped rope in front of the mirror. Five local boys sat in the bleachers wearing street clothes and two had gym bags on their laps. Each boy in turn gave me the stink eye. The smallest boy chewed gum and squeezed a rubber ball. "What school ya go?" he asked me.

"Punahou."

"What? Ya like beef, ya fuckin' haole?"

"Step into the ring, pal," I said.

The boy sprang off the bleachers and swung a wild left. I bobbed and threw a right lead that hit him flush in the jaw. The boy stumbled backwards and tripped on the mat.

"Fuckin' haole," he said when he got up, "ya wen' cut ma fuckin' tongue!" He moved his tongue around and blood dribbled out of his mouth.

Da Battlah jump-roped his way over. "Break it up."

The boy spit blood on the mat. "Dis fucka go

Punahou," he told Da Battlah, "he stay trespassin' on Farrington."

"This gym's for everyone," Da Battlah replied.

"Dis none of yoa business, Blackie."

Da Battlah dropped the rope and grabbed the boy by his shirt. "I'm making it my business, punk."

The boy returned to the bleachers and Da Battlah resumed his skipping.

"Where's Mr. Clean?" I asked.

"Hollywood," Da Battlah replied.

I made my way around the ring. Uncle Sharkey was on one knee filling up bottles at a faucet. He still had on the fedora but this time his jacket was blue.

"Hey, Uncle Sharkey," I said, "congratulations."

"Foa what?"

"Tiny won."

"He did what I tol' um."

"Who are those boys in the bleachers?"

Sharkey capped a full bottle with a stopper and started filling a second. "Keeds always show up afta fight night," he said. "T'ink dey can do it all in one day."

"Do what?"

"What else? Be champ of da world." He gazed over at the bleachers. "If ya keeds wanna learn to fight," he said, "start by moppin' da mats. Mop an' bucket stay in da locka room."

The boy who'd swung at me stood up. "I like fight, not mop."

"Get los'," Sharkey said.

"Fuck off, Gramps."

Da Battlah threw down his rope and headed for the bleachers. The boy saw him coming and ran down the wooden steps. The double doors flew open and the boy was gone.

Sharkey turned off the water and capped the second bottle. "Who's moppin'?" he asked.

The boys looked at one another and filed silently out of the gym. The doors shut and the gym was as quiet as a church. Doves cooed in the rafters.

"Punks get one t'ing in common," Sharkey said.

"What's that?" I asked.

He stood and jammed a long finger into my chest. "No heart. Plenny can dish, few can take. Know why no monsta heavyweights?"

"Why?"

"Big buggahs make good cowards."

"Really?"

Sharkey nodded. "Man wit' heart cut um in half. Dempsey wen' smash up dat giant, Primo Canera. Man wit' heart cheats Faddah Time. Lookit Ezzard Charles."

I picked up the water bottles and carried them over to the ring. I wasn't sure who these boxers were, but it sounded good. That day, Sharkey threw out a list of names, a Who's Who in the boxing world, complete with corresponding truths and maxims. Then came a litany of Dos and Don'ts, some which didn't even apply to me. Da Battlah stopped pounding the heavy bag and shadowboxed his way over to listen. Here's what Sharkey said:

1. Listen to lots of music, especially Frank Sinatra.
2. Don't blink when a punch is coming.
3. Don't train the day before the fight.
4. Don't exploit a weakness all at once.
5. Spit to lose weight.
6. Don't screw the day of the fight.
7. Eat rice to prevent farting.
8. Pet cats for good luck.
9. Don't lift weights—big muscles slow you down.
10. Watch your opponent's eyes, not his gloves.

*   *   *

Wayne wasn't in any of my classes. I crossed paths with him occasionally at the snack shop next to Dole Cafeteria. He had freshmen boys carry his lunch tray around a banyan tree and, if they dropped anything, he made them buy him Creamsicles and Sidewalk Sundaes. If they refused, he'd give them the choice of either standing on their head or eating a knuckle sandwich. If they stood on their heads, Wayne poured milk or juice down the legs of their pants. One day I saw him sitting at a snack shop table across from Jay Pearsons, a pale boy with droopy eyelids whose role in volleyball was to set up shots for Wayne to spike. Their team had just been invited to the state tournament. Wayne had rice balls on his plate and he threw them at two underclassmen sharing an HP-35 calculator. A rice ball hit one of the boys in the head and they ran off.

I walked over to Wayne. "Pick on someone your own size," I said.

Wayne put his elbow down and reached across the table. "You're not my size, Squirt."

Jay grabbed Wayne's hand and they began arm-wrestling.

"What's your bag, man?" I pressed.

"Take a whiz, Squirt."

"The bigger they are," I said, "the harder they fall."

Wayne slammed Jay's hand down on the table. He stood up and crossed his arms in front of his chest.

"Better run, Jeff," Jay advised, "run for the hills."

Wayne shoved me and I flew back into a table.

"Quit it," a girl said, "you nearly spilled my chocolate milk."

I walked up to Wayne and shoved him back—he barely moved. He stood there smiling and put up his fists.

I took the boxer's stance I'd learned at the gym, with my elbows in against my sides and my hands protecting my face. I watched Wayne's eyes, not his fists.

Wayne threw a left at my face that I dodged easily. He tried tagging me with a right but my hand was up to deflect it. I jogged out into the open and waited next to the banyan tree.

"Chicken," Jay said, "puck, puck, puck!"

I put up my fists. "Right now."

Wayne walked out into the sunlight. "This is gonna be fun," he said.

"Fight!" Jay announced.

Boys and girls in the snack shop and Dole Cafeteria hustled out to watch. Everyone crowded around the banyan tree.

Wayne put up his fists and charged so I backed up to the trunk. He threw a left that hit my chest and a right that just missed my head. I countered with a right jab that grazed his jaw.

"That supposed to hurt?" Wayne asked.

"Love tap," said Jay.

Wayne faked a right and, when I reached up to intercept it, he hit me in the nose with a left. The blow didn't stun me because he hadn't put his weight behind it. I fired off a right lead but he backed away and my punch fell short. Wayne moved in closer. I was sure he'd unload a flurry of shots so I kept my elbows in and my fists up.

"That's enough!" a man said. Dean McQueen jogged over and stood between us. "Everyone except these two clowns back to lunch," he ordered.

The boys and girls skulked back to the cafeteria and the snack shop.

"I ate already," Jay told McQueen.

"Eat again, Jay," McQueen said, "you'll need plenty of energy if you plan on defending our title."

Jay stuck his hands in his pockets and left.

McQueen stood there in his Aloha shirt with his arms crossed. He was a stocky man with sideburns and hairy forearms. He seemed more like a police captain than a dean. "How's the ol' volleyball arm, Wayne?" he asked.

"I was just exercising it."

McQueen patted Wayne on the shoulder. "I want you to win us that championship next Saturday."

"Make room in the trophy case," Wayne replied.

McQueen stared at me. "You're barking up the wrong tree, sonny boy."

"But Wayne started it."

"I don't care who started it," McQueen said. "But I do care about what kind of example you're setting. These underclassmen look to seniors for guidance and advice."

"What's wrong with fighting back?" I asked.

"Back to lunch before you're suspended."

I returned to the snack shop and ordered a mahimahi sandwich with fries. I'd spent four years in high school at Punahou and my class dean didn't know my name. It would have been different if I had been a star athlete or an award-winning scholar. Instead, I was "sonny boy." I sat at the table farthest away from Wayne. But it wasn't long before he strolled by with Jay.

Wayne put a lunch tray down on my table. "Okay, Squirt," he said, "as punishment, I want you to run this tray twice around upper field track."

"I wanna box you," I said.

Wayne slammed his fist into my mahimahi sandwich. "I got news," he said, "you're no boxer."

"I'll fight you at Waialae Golf Course," I replied, "after school next Friday."

Friday was the second round of the Hawaiian Open. But I knew "after school" meant we'd be there after Jack Nicklaus and Arnold Palmer completed the 18th hole.

Wayne put up his fists. "Bare knuckles right now."

"Ben wants to film the fight for his Video class."

Wayne put down his hands. He smiled and whispered something in Jay's ear and they both laughed. Wayne blushed and rubbed his face. "I'll drive you like a golf ball, Squirt."

"And I'll broke yoa face," I fired back.

"Gee, I'm shivering in my boots."

"You'll show?"

Wayne nodded. "We'll have an ambulance standing by for you."

"That golf course is a big place," Jay said.

"14th hole," I replied, "five sharp."

Wayne threw out a jab. "Wouldn't miss it for the world."

*   *   *

I trained hard after school with Uncle Sharkey. I learned how to skip rope and hit the heavy bag. I couldn't figure out the speed bag because my impatience hurt my timing. Part of my workout meant sparring with Tiny. I went from probably the worst fighter on Oahu to someone who understood the basics. I realized I could take a punch when Tiny whacked me but didn't knock me out.

Sharkey shadowboxed constantly. He threw out fists like pistons, shooting long straight jabs at the mirror. He feigned and dodged punches. He bobbed and weaved. Sometimes I'd catch him staring off into space and mumbling profanities, as if remembering the blow-by-blow of an old bootleg fight. Gramma had said he'd taken incredible punishment in his day. Once I walked up to him and he didn't see me—a few minutes passed and he held out one of his arms. "Feel dat," he said.

I squeezed his forearm. "Feels like a rock."

"Dat's from hana."

*   *   *

Two days before my fight with Wayne, Tiny returned to the gym to start training for his next fight. He'd moved up in rank and was listed in the Top Ten for middleweights. I watched him work the speed bag—he moved the bag around the platform by striking it with short jabs and tapping it with his forearms and elbows.

"You had a great fight at the HIC," I told Tiny.

He stepped away from the bag. "Like try?"

I stepped under the platform and struck the bag. It wobbled like a wounded duck.

"Not hard," Tiny said. "Tap um."

"Hey, Tiny," I said tapping the bag, "is Sharkey pupule?"

"Sharkey stay one prince," he responded, "an' no forget dat." Tiny told me he'd been dealing drugs on Hotel Street when Sharkey found him and helped turn his life around. He needed to make up for lost time if he was ever going to get a shot at the world title. "My faddah like me foa be docta," he admitted.

"You take care of people," I said, "only in a different way."

Sharkey walked over. "Quit gabbin' an' get in da ring, Punahou."

It was time to spar. Tiny and I slipped on our gloves and Sharkey cinched them up. It was my last day at the gym and I wanted to show Sharkey I could fight. I slipped through the ropes knowing I had the reach advantage. If I kept Tiny away with jabs, I'd make it through the round. Tiny hadn't been going one hundred percent but he wasn't pulling his punches either. He climbed into the ring and shadowboxed in the opposite corner.

"Beef," Sharkey said.

I danced around Tiny and, when he came in, I flicked out my right.

"No respec' um," Sharkey told me.

It was hard not to respect Tiny seeing he'd knocked out a ranked fighter. He came in close and I danced away. I had a slight advantage because I was a lefty and it was natural for me to move to his left, away from his power. He hit me with a glancing blow to the head and I threw a weak right. He countered with four straight shots to my belly and I was on the canvas.

"Get up, Punahou."

I looked up—doves were looking down from their perches in the rafters. They looked so peaceful up there that I wanted to stare up at them until the round was over. Something floated into my view and, when I focused, I saw the eye of the peacock feather glinting on Sharkey's hat.

"Get up!" Sharkey said. "No Gill goes down li' dat."

I got back up and stumbled around the ring. Tiny charged in. I felt groggy but managed to throw a right that hit Tiny's chin and a left that flew over his head. He fired a scorching right to my solar plexus and I bounced against the ropes.

"Finish da bum," Sharkey said.

Tiny came in for the kill but I slipped away along the ropes. He charged ahead and cornered me again. He came in with his head low and I crouched and threw a strange punch that seemed somehow natural—it was between a hook and an uppercut and it looped up at a forty-five degree angle. It hit Tiny square in the jaw.

"To da moon!" Sharkey cheered.

Tiny raised his eyebrows. He battered me with both hands and backed me up into the ropes. I tried fighting off the ropes but lost my leverage and he hooked me hard to the head and I dropped to one knee.

"Pau hana," Sharkey said.

I got up and leaned against the ropes.

Sharkey made his way around the ring. "Good one!" he said. "Ya wen' connec' wit' da kine bolo punch."

"What's that?"

"Whacha wen' hit um wit'," he said. He took off his fedora and rested it on the turnbuckle. His gray hair was slicked back with hair cream and his ears were so cauliflowered they resembled flower bulbs. "Dat bolo hurt, Tiny?"

"Nah."

"No lie," Sharkey said. "Kid Gavilan t'rew da bolo."

Tiny climbed out of the ring and pulled off his gloves with his teeth. "Was good kine punch," he said and made his way over to the padded bench. "Show um now?" Tiny asked Sharkey.

"Show um."

Tiny reached into his gym bag and pulled out a pair of black trunks. He held them up—"The Rainbow Warrior" was stitched in white on the left leg and there was a rainbow behind it.

"Those are for me?"

Tiny nodded. "My girlfriend get da kine machine."

"Ya know dis volleyball punk?" Sharkey asked me.

"Yeah?"

Sharkey ran his hand through his hair and put his fedora back on. "Break his frickin' hat."

*   *   *

Speedy promoted my beef with Wayne as "The Fight of the Century" and more than fifty guys from Punahou showed up at Waialae Golf Course after school. Hugh had gotten everyone to chip in to buy a keg of Primo and pupus. The blast from an airhorn would signal the beginning and end of each round. We were to go three rounds of three minutes each. Two garden hoses were stretched around four coconut trees on the 14th hole, compliments of George and Speedy. The trees weren't cornered right so the ring resembled a parallelogram. Kaipo Dudoit, the hapa haole mike man for the cheerleaders, had volunteered to ref. Ben filmed the pre-fight beer chugging and impromptu sumo wrestling on the putting green. The beer, cone sushi, and manapua were going fast.

I made my way through the crowd. Steve was waiting for me in the ring and I slipped between the hoses. He wrapped gauze around my hands, placed squares of foam over my knuckles, and taped the foam on.

"I should sell my stash," he said cinching up my red Everlast gloves.

"Can't you stop thinking about drugs for one minute?" I asked.

"I need bread for college."

The sun filtered through the coconut trees and the ring was a battlefield of light and shadow. I bounced up and down in my sneakers. The grass felt like carpet. A white mansion with a blue-tiled roof stood next to the course and beyond that was the ocean. I pounded my gloves together and wondered if Wayne could take a punch. I was prepared to take his best shots and deliver a few of my own.

Steve leaned against the hoses and sneezed. "Gotta take my medicine," he said and pulled out a vial of hash oil, a glass straw, and his Bic lighter. He flicked on the lighter and heated the bottom of the vial. He sucked up the fumes through the glass straw and I smelled the sharpness of the oil. He offered me the vial.

I pounded my gloves together.

Steve sucked at the straw. "Ah," he said, "this helps with allergies."

A trumpet blared the Punahou fight song. Wayne paraded across the golf course with an entourage of friends, including Coop, Jay, and the Twinkies. Wayne wore orange trunks and white Adidas running shoes. His hands were wrapped in wads of gauze and strips of tape and he held them over his head. Red boxing gloves were slung over Jay's shoulder and the Twinkies carried water bottles.

Ben darted over with his video camera. "What's the prediction, Wayne?"

Wayne shuffled his feet like Ali. "Won't it be fun, K-O Squirt in one."

"What's your training method?"

"Pot, booze, and bimbos."

The guys laughed and booed.

Wayne jogged over and stood outside the ring. He tested the strength of the hoses and fired off combinations in rapid succession. A Twinkie squirted water in his mouth. Jay massaged Wayne's shoulders and Coop put on his gloves. Wayne ducked under the top hose and entered the ring. "What's it say on his trunks?" he asked squinting at me.

The other Twinkie looked across the ring. "The Rainbow Warrior."

"Hey, Squirt," Wayne called, "I'll knock rainbows outta your ass!"

The boys on Wayne's side of the ring chuckled. Most were Jocks from the volleyball team and they were wearing their Punahou jerseys. They were an arrogant bunch who enjoyed humiliating teams from the OIA, the association of public schools.

The boys on my side looked worried, especially Hugh and Speedy. George seemed ready to leave. A group of timid boys huddled beside a kiawe tree—Wayne had bullied them all. I had a sick feeling in the pit of my stomach I'd get knocked out and disappoint everyone.

Wayne fired off a second salvo of punches and his

face turned red from holding his breath. A Twinkie offered him a cup of water and he punched it out of his hand. Wayne grabbed the top hose and started doing squats.

Kaipo blew the airhorn and Wayne bounded out of his corner. We met at the center of the ring and Wayne stared down at me.

"Whoever leaves the ring," Kaipo said, "loses."

"What if I knock him through the hoses?" Wayne asked.

"Same rules as Honolulu All-Star Wrestling," Kaipo explained, "you've got twenty seconds to climb back in. Now touch gloves and return to your corners until the horn sounds."

Wayne and I gave each other the stink eye. We touched gloves, he faked a right, and I ducked.

"Sucker!" Wayne said.

We returned to our corners.

Steve climbed out of the ring and leaned against a coconut tree. "Remember the Alamo," he said.

The airhorn screeched. Wayne jogged over and met me on my side of the ring. He threw wild rights and lefts that I dodged. He hit me with a right hook I didn't see coming but I countered with a left that snapped his head back. The guys hooted and hollered. Wayne was right-handed so I slipped to his left, away from his right. He charged like a bull, clinched, and punched me twice in the back of the neck.

Kaipo separated us. "No rabbit punches!"

Wayne charged again and I danced away. The grass

felt good and I was surprised how light I was on my feet. Ben knelt down with his video camera—he stuck the lens between the hoses to get a better angle. Wayne threw a left that missed my head and I moved out of his reach.

"Chicken!" Jay said.

Wayne charged a third time. I stood my ground and threw a left at his face point blank, putting my weight behind the punch. I connected and the blow sent him reeling backwards. His arms moved like windmills and he fell back against the hoses. The guys on my side of the ring cheered.

"Knock 'im out!" Hugh said.

"Break his face!" said Speedy.

Wayne stared out at the crowd trying to determine who'd spoken. The guys pressed in close and some rested their arms over the top hose. Wayne charged a fourth time and threw a left that narrowly missed my jaw. He was winding up with his right when I tagged him with an overhand left to the face. He lurched back into the far corner and grabbed the trunk of a coconut tree. "Fuck!" Wayne said. He put a glove to his nose to check for blood.

"Watch his left," Coop said. "Jeff's a lefty!"

Wayne measured me with his jab. I continued circling to his weak side, keeping him off balance with rights. Most of my punches were connecting because his hands were down. I hit his belly with a right lead and slammed a straight left to his jaw. The airhorn sounded— I returned to my corner knowing I'd won the first round.

"Primo beef," Steve told me before wandering off

across the green.

Kaipo came over. "You okay, Jeff?"

I pounded my gloves together. "Never better."

"It's going to get tougher," Kaipo warned. "Now he knows you're a southpaw."

"He's not going to knock me out."

Kaipo nodded and walked over to the other corner. Wayne looked confused. His face was red and dripping sweat. A Twinkie squirted water in his mouth. I realized this fight had a lot to do with me losing Debbie Mills in junior high. But it wasn't all about her. I was fighting for the boys Wayne had pushed around for years. I spotted Steve smoking a joint out on the fairway—it was his famous Thai Stick dipped in opium.

"Steve," I said.

He swung an imaginary club at the 14th hole and strolled over to the flag. He took a puff and lined up his putt.

"Steve!"

He putted an imaginary ball and puffed his way on to the 15th. The airhorn sounded and I knew I'd lost my cornerman.

In the second round, Wayne changed tactics—he stood back and battered me with long jabs. I danced around trying to throw off his timing but he continued landing lefts to my face and body. He punished me with his reach advantage. Whenever I got in close, he shot out a left. My legs felt rubbery. We clinched and Wayne rested all his weight on me. "You're history, Squirt," he said and pushed me in the chest with his open gloves. I dropped my hands and he hit me in the head with a right cross that stunned me.

"Yes!" Jay cheered.

The airhorn blared—the second round belonged to Wayne. I headed to my corner and leaned against the hoses. I felt woozy. It seemed as if the world beyond the ring was under water. Speedy came over and told me to bob and weave and to go to the body with my left. Jay and Coop shouted instructions at Wayne. His orange trunks were dark with sweat. I thought about Debbie Mills. I imagined her dancing in a chiffon dress at her prom while the band played "The Yellow Rose of Texas."

The airhorn sounded.

In the third and final round, we circled each another. I was saving the little energy I had left for a final flurry.

"I'm knocking you out, asshole," Wayne said. He was looking for that one opening to end the fight. He faked a right and I went up to block it. His left smacked my temple.

"Kill 'im!" said Jay.

Wayne could hurt me if I didn't keep my gloves up and elbows in. But he was tiring too. I glanced past the top hose and saw Chip Morningstar and Bernie Fredman. Wayne had made it his annual tradition to write "To a Real Panty Waist" in Chip's yearbook. He'd told Bernie his nose was big because air was free. I spotted Ken Ito—Wayne had humiliated him at our sophomore class picnic by yanking off his trunks and making him run naked past the girls. I summoned my strength and threw a right that fell short. Wayne countered with a left that sailed over my head. I got in close, crouched down, and swung my left up in an arc. I delivered a bolo punch that struck Wayne in the heart. He winced and backed up. It was against the hoses that I threw a second bolo that looped over his right shoulder and banged his head with such force that it felt as if I'd busted my hand. He had to hold on to the hoses to keep from falling.

"Rainbow Warrior," Bernie said, "Rainbow Warrior!"

A third bolo hit his glove. My hands were down and Wayne blasted me with a straight right to the jaw that nearly tore my head off—it was easily his best punch of the fight. A cheer went up from Wayne's side and the airhorn sounded.

I looked into the crowd and saw fear in the eyes of my classmates. I pulled off my gloves with my teeth as a trio of husky haoles on golf carts surrounded the ring. "Hawaiian Open" was printed on their shirts. They sprang off their carts and the biggest one yanked down the top hose.

"Beat it," the biggest said, "buncha punks."

"Already called Five-O," said the second.

The third nodded. "That keg's mine."

Ben entered the ring and filmed Wayne. "Who won?" Ben asked.

"Duh," Wayne said.

"Where's the knock out?"

"Fuck you, dimwit."

Jay pulled off Wayne's gloves and a Twinkie removed the tape and gauze.

Kaipo looked into the camera. "Wayne won that fight," he said and raised Wayne's arm.

Speedy glared at Kaipo. "Bullshit."

Seeing Wayne standing there with his arm raised made me feel like barfing. I looked toward the ocean. The trade winds were picking up and white caps broke over the water. A man stood on the balcony of the white mansion. He had binoculars. He was probably the one who'd notified security. He put the binoculars down and I swore it was Arnold Palmer.

"Good fight," Kaipo told me as he helped George and Speedy roll up the hoses.

"What?" I asked. "You said I lost."

"Yeah," Kaipo replied, "but I think you hurt him."

*   *   *

News of the fight spread through campus. Chip Morningstar called me "the Champ." Ken Ito said he'd will me a match with Ali. Speedy told everyone I deserved a rematch. A few Jocks nodded when I walked by their benches in front of Cooke Library. I was surprised when Coop and a Twinkie congratulated me on a great fight.

I received a note during English class to report to Dean McQueen's office at fourth period. URGENT was scrawled on the top of the note. McQueen wasn't my favorite person on campus, especially after my mandatory college conference. He had told me I would never get into a mainland college because of my poor grades and low SAT scores. He'd suggested a career in auto repair or welding. But I'd taken Hoagie's advice and applied to the University of Colorado. To my surprise, I'd gotten on their waiting list and two weeks later received an acceptance letter with the school's gold seal. My father was pleased but he said it was still a far cry from Amherst or Stanford.

The bell for fourth period rang and I climbed the stairs to McQueen's office in Alexander Hall. I walked past a case on the second floor crammed with trophies and pictures of past champions. Some of the football players wore leather helmets.

McQueen's door was to the right of the stairway. The door had a smoked glass panel. I had a bad feeling about this. I tapped on the glass.

"Jeff Gill?"

"Yes."

"Get in here!"

I was surprised he hadn't called me "sonny boy." I opened the door and McQueen stood at his office window. My file was scattered over his desk—he'd flipped through the scores, report cards, class rankings, and teacher comments that defined my high school existence.

"Shut that door and plant your skinny butt," McQueen said.

I closed the door and sat. A potted, leafless ficus was wedged between two file cabinets and a carnation lei that had turned brown hung off the doorknob to the adjoining room.

McQueen wore a short sleeve shirt and a wide tie

with yellow and blue stripes. He smelled like Aqua Velva. For the first time I noticed crow's feet around his eyes and a hula girl tattoo on his right bicep. Pictures of him and his Army buddies were on the wall. There was one photo of him posing at the sign for the 38th Parallel wearing sunglasses like General MacArthur. McQueen remained at the window and studied the courtyard. "Know what you are, Gill?" he asked.

I shook my head.

"A dope. But I don't know who's worse, you or your brother."

"What's wrong with Ben?"

"Punahou didn't hold him back for nothing. Now he doesn't have the grades to graduate."

"Can't you get him a tutor or something?"

"Look, Gill," said McQueen, "I'll cut to the chase. You're the reason we lost the state championship to Waianae."

"How'd I do that?"

He sat in his chair and plucked a volleyball off his desk. "By bruising Wayne Braswell's esophagus. You took the leap outta our greatest leaper."

"Oh, my god," I said, "you're the coach."

"Of course I'm the coach. And I plan on expelling you for assault and battery."

"But I'm graduating."

He slammed the ball down on his desk. "Not anymore."

Now that Dean McQueen was aware I existed, he

wanted to boot me out. My chance to attend a mainland university was going down the toilet. I imagined my father's face swelling to one hundred times its normal size—the face floated off his shoulders and hovered over Diamond Head crater. "Cheesus Holy Mother of Christ!" the monstrous mouth said and the volcano erupted.

"I've already discussed this matter with administration," McQueen continued, "and tomorrow I take it to President Young."

"But Wayne wanted to fight."

"Now why don't I believe you, Gill?" McQueen asked swiveling in his chair. "You've hurt Punahou by what you've done," he lectured, "and there's a price to pay."

"There's a film."

He stopped swiveling and frowned. The crow's feet became more pronounced. "I didn't hear anything about a film."

"It shows two consenting seniors boxing in a ring. I don't think those are grounds to expel me. But if you try, my father will sue both you and Punahou, Queeny."

His bicep tensed and the breasts on the hula girl grew. "What the hell did you call me?"

"Queeny."

"I want that film on my desk today, you little prick."

"I don't have it."

He drummed his fingers on the desk. "Who does?"

I stood up. "I can't reveal the name, Queeny," I said, "in order to protect the innocent."

He picked a pencil off of his desk and snapped it in

half with his thumb. "Get outta my office, Gill, " he said. "Go on, get the hell out!"

*   *   *

Ben said I'd put up a good fight but that I lost it at the end when Wayne tagged me with the shot to the jaw. "That was the clincher," Ben said. "Unreal you didn't go down."

"What about my bolo punches?"

"They don't show up too good on the film."

My father ran into Mr. Braswell on the steps of the courthouse and Mr. Braswell said, "Wayne beat the Holy bejesus outta Jeff."

The room was packed the day Ben showed the film to his Video class. He'd wanted to hire a hooker to hold up round cards but lost his nerve. But Ben did serve popcorn, peanuts, and soft drinks like the fights at the HIC. The class booed and cheered during the fight. Curious students peered in from the hallway. The film featured close-ups of Wayne's okole in his wet trunks and a great zoom in of me stunning him with a left in the first round. Mr. Meecham gave Ben an A-minus for "conflict, humor, and point-of-view." That was the highest mark Ben had ever received at Punahou and exactly what he needed to graduate.

LAURA KWON

Laura Kwon was an enigma. She had a slight build and delicate features but she wasn't weak. She was lean and strong and walked with an assertive sexuality. She wore sleeveless dresses with Mandarin collars and her hair fell like a shiny black river down to her waist. She held out her shoulders like wings and that made me think she would do great things with her life. She was a sprinter on the girls' track team and had smashed Hawaii State records for the 100-yard dash and the 440. Her independent nature sent the message that not only could she survive not being popular but that she preferred it. She usually had a wry smile whenever she strolled through campus.

"Stuck up chick," said Coop.

Wesley nodded. "She needs it."

The Jocks were threatened by Laura's record-breaking performances. Her conservative nature made her unpopular with the Surfers and Druggies. The Brains didn't appreciate her competitive spark. Even boys at the bottom of the social totem pole considered her distant and unapproachable. The Party Girls thought she was a snob. She'd run for student body president and lost by a landslide. But Laura wasn't concerned with the politics of popularity. She cultivated detachment while her peers pursued acceptance and approval. Failing didn't bother her—it just rolled off her like water.

Laura and I were in Miss Takata's English class. I'd helped her with a paper on John Steinbeck's *In Dubious Battle* and she rewarded me with a twenty-dollar gift certificate to Ming Kim III, a Korean restaurant owned by her father. Her parents were first generation Koreans who'd fled Seoul when Mao Tse-tung's Red Army surprised America's divisions on Thanksgiving Day in 1950.

A week after my fight with Wayne, Laura and I walked out of English class into the courtyard fronting Alexander Hall. "Heard about you boxing," she said. "It's not good getting hit in the head, Jeff."

"I had to do it."

Laura wrinkled her brow. "Forced into fisticuffs?"

"Something like that," I said. "Can I ask a personal question?"

"Absolutely."

"Are you going to the prom?"

Laura stopped beside a plumeria tree and held her books in front of her with both hands. That wry smile returned. "Why? Are you asking, Jeff?"

"Well, yeah. I mean, if you haven't been asked."

"Why me?"

"Because I like you."

"That's not the reason."

"No?"

She shook her head and her hair moved back and forth over her shoulders. "You're asking because someone already turned you down."

"I haven't asked anyone but you."

She looked up at the sky and the gold of her Mandarin collar glimmered in the sunlight. "This sounds serious."

"I can be un-serious," I said reaching up to pluck a pink plumeria off the tree.

Laura laughed. "That's not a word."

"Poetic license."

"My mother wouldn't approve."

"I'm not asking your mother," I said handing her the flower, "I'm asking you."

She placed the flower behind her right ear. "Okay, Jeff. You got me."

To my amazement, Laura agreed to go. The agreement seemed more amicable than romantic, a platonic way to share in the final love dance of our fellow seniors. But I had not ruled out romance. I thought the atmosphere of the prom and the fact we were graduating might bring us together. I felt rejuvenated after my fight and being accepted by a mainland university.

The future was exciting and ripe with possibilities.

*   *   *

The night of the prom, I parked my B-210 in front of Laura's house in Palolo Valley. I got out wearing my blue graduation blazer, buff tie, and gray slacks. I held an orchid wrist corsage in its plastic container and walked by an open garage with Shell No-Pest Strips dangling from the ceiling. A black Lincoln Continental with "Ming Kim III" plates was parked in the garage. Flip-flops, sandals, and shoes were stacked on a strip of Astroturf beside the front door. I rang the bell.

A woman opened the door only wide enough to stick her head out. She wore glasses and her hair was in a bun. "Who dis?" she asked.

"Mrs. Kwon?"

"How ya know me?"

"I'm Jeff."

"Who?"

"Jeff Gill. I'm taking Laura to the prom?"

"Ya no sound so shoo-ah."

"I'm sure."

"Ya playboy?"

A hand appeared over her head and pried the door open. Mrs. Kwon disappeared and Laura stood in the doorway wearing a sleeveless white holoku gown. The hemline was mid-thigh and she wore white gloves. The gloves accentuated her tan arms and shoulders. Three strands of pikake looped across her chest. She looked like an angel. "Hi, Jeff," she said.

"Hi."

"Is that for me?" she asked pointing to the corsage.

"Oh, yeah," I said and handed it to her.

Mrs. Kwon peered over her shoulder. "Wheah da ring?"

Laura rolled her eyes. "We're not engaged, Ma."

"Look like to me."

"Come inside, Jeff," Laura said.

I pulled off my loafers and placed them on the Astroturf. Ma returned to the doorway and stepped aside to let me pass. She wore a pink muumuu and chartreuse socks. The room was full of cherrywood chests with gold and silver latches. Bamboo scrolls with brush paintings covered the walls. Most of the scrolls depicted idyllic harvests and rolling mountains but I saw one of a man navigating a boat through huge swells. Men laughed in the back room and it smelled like cigars. Pa, Laura's father, was playing mahjong with men from the restaurant. He was not to be disturbed.

"Ai-ya," a man said in the back room, "ya kook!"

"Cheatah!" another replied.

Tiles shuffled on the game board. Someone cleared his throat and spat.

"Pa loves to gamble," Laura said.

Ma nodded. "Big stakes." She ran to the stove and stirred a pot. "Hum ha poak," she told me. "Ya like?"

"I would," I said, "but there's food at the prom."

"Latah?"

"That'd be great."

Ma pulled a butcher knife off a rack and began chopping green onions. Bottles of soy, hoi sin, and oyster sauce rested on the wooden counter. Ma finished chopping. She gathered up the chopped onions and dropped them in the pot. She stirred the simmering pork and onions with a large wooden spoon and grabbed the bottle of oyster sauce. She slapped the bottom of the bottle and sauce squirted into the pot. The aroma of pork, onions, and oyster sauce made my stomach growl.

Laura popped open the container and fastened the corsage to her wrist. "No ka oi," she said turning her wrist back and forth. "Look, Ma."

"Look costly," Ma said.

Laura smiled. "Mahalo, Jeff." She opened the fridge and pulled out a maile lei. She was taller than I remembered and I noticed she had on a pair of white wedgees. She draped the maile lei over my shoulders and gave me a peck on the cheek.

"Thanks," I said.

"Ma helped me."

"Wheah da hum ha!" came a voice from the back room.

"Quiet, Pa," Ma said.

"Bring be-ah too!"

Ma delivered bottles of Kirin beer and a steaming plate of hum ha pork over glass noodles to the back room. She returned and watched me slip on my loafers at the doorway. Ma followed us out. I opened the car door for Laura before climbing into the driver's seat. Ma stood on the curb in her socks shaking her butcher knife. "No drinkin'!"

Laura rolled down the passenger window. "Goodnight, Ma."

*   *   *

I drove Laura to the Oahu Country Club, a private establishment not far from the Pali. Its driveway was lined with macadamia trees. We passed a lava fountain and I parked beside a lehua grove.

We got out and I touched a red blossom. A legend promised rain if you pulled a flower from the lehua tree. "Should I pull?" I asked Laura.

"Have an umbrella?"

I pulled the blossom off the branch.

Laura took my arm and I escorted her through a foyer of potted palms and paintings of whale hunts off Lahaina. There was also a painting of Captain Cook's arrival on the Big Island—outrigger canoes in Kealakekua Bay surrounded the *HMS Discovery*. A band sang "I Heard It Through the Grapevine" in the ballroom and the lead singer resembled Tina Turner. "The Lava Gods" was printed on their base drum. Couples were already dancing. Color wheels were aimed up at a rotating disco ball that reflected back dots of colored light. The aroma of plumeria, carnation, and pikake filled the room. George walked by with Dawn. Hugh and Lucy waited in line for the buffet and teachers huddled at tables around the dance floor. Girls wearing carnation leis sat with men in Marine uniforms. We stood next to a mermaid sculpted in ice and watched the dancers: Brian spun Evelyn Chau from the Pep Club; Wesley wore a silver three-piece suit and danced with

Monica; Mr. Farley did the Twist with Miss Meyer. It seemed funny without Ben there. He was back home drinking Primo with his friend Mike Swenson because they'd both waited too long to ask anyone and then decided Punahou girls were snobs. Wayne wasn't there either—he'd told Ben he had "a hot date" with a stripper from the Glade Swing Club.

I spotted an empty table with an arrangement of pink antheriums, red torch ginger, and ferns. We took the table and, after a few songs, The Lava Gods took a break.

"What's your favorite song?" I asked Laura.

"Anything by Cecilio and Kapono."

"What do you think of the prom so far?"

"It blows my mind."

"How come?"

"They're trying so hard to be who they are on campus."

"Know what I like about you?"

"What?"

"You say what's on your mind."

Laura smiled. "Thought guys hated that."

"Not so far."

Someone outside tapped on the glass door next to our table. It was Steve. He wore an Aloha shirt with white pants and a girl was with him. He opened the door—his eyes were glassy and he reeked of pakalolo. "Joe Frazier!" he said and walked in with Heidi Shigemoto, a cheerleader for the Kalani Falcons. Heidi wore a red micromini and white knee-high boots. After introductions, Steve sat on the other side of Laura and Heidi knelt on the carpet next to my chair.

"Jeff and me," Steve told Laura, "we started a club."

"Which one?" Laura asked.

"The Drug Club."

"Steve's just kidding," I said.

Steve pulled out a doobie from his shirt pocket and waved it at Laura. "Toke?"

Laura crossed her legs and jiggled her foot. "Not right now."

"I get da royal munchies from da kine," Heidi giggled.

"They've got mahimahi and grasshopper pie," I said.

Heidi licked her lips and poked me with her elbow. "Ya stay one fighta, eh?"

"Yeah," I said, " and Steve's my cornerman, I mean, when he's not busy golfing."

Heidi looked at Steve. "Ya neva wen' tell me dat, Sweety."

Steve studied the disco ball. "Musta slipped my mind."

The Lava Gods returned to the stage and they opened with Cecilio and Kapono's "Sunshine Love."

"I've gotta dance," Laura said.

Heidi jumped up and kicked one leg over her head. "Let's go, gangeys!"

Steve shook his head. "Count me out," he said. "I'm wasted."

Heidi grabbed his hand and pulled him out of his

seat. "No act haole style."

We all danced to "Sunshine Love." The song had a fast beat with melancholy interludes. It was about a noncommittal girl and a boy trying to win her over. Laura did a few spins on her own and started a rock 'n' roll version of the hula. I danced around her. We changed partners and Heidi bounced up and down as if she was riding a pogo stick. Steve put his hands on Laura's waist but she brushed them off as the song ended.

"We go eat!" Heidi said.

We headed over to a buffet table with mounds of almond mahimahi and black pepper steak. Speedy was piling his plate high. Bernie came over and said I was probably a Roman gladiator in a past life. Laura told me she wasn't hungry so we watched Steve and Heidi stack their plates with slabs of mahimahi, steak, rice pilaf, and bow-tie pasta.

"My makas stay biggah dan my stomach," Heidi confessed in the buffet line.

Steve picked up a filet of mahimahi and dipped it in a pool of tartar sauce on his salad plate. "I'll grind what you don't," he told Heidi and folded the filet into his mouth.

"No be one pig, Sweety," Heidi said.

Steve swallowed and burped. "Oink, oink."

Laura took my hand and led me back to the dance floor. A Twinkie was dancing with Mindy Birch and he passed around a bottle of cherry vodka. Hugh handed me the bottle and I took a swig. Laura and I danced to everything from "Paint It Black" to "Superstition." We danced closer and got rhythm as a couple. She giggled when I slid on an orchid that had fallen off Lucy's lei. The Lava Gods started singing "Killing Me Softly With His Song" and the couples going steady hugged. Lucy was with Hugh now and I envied the way they held one another as dots of colored light glided over them. Laura watched with a sad detachment.

"Wanna slow dance?" I asked.

"Let's sit this one out," she said and walked off.

I went after her and caught her next to the ice mermaid. I watched her pluck petals off her corsage and drop them on the carpet.

"This was a big mistake," Laura told me.

"Why?"

"I'm not your girlfriend, Jeff."

"I know that."

"But that's what 'slow dance' means."

"You can slow dance without being in love."

Laura adjusted her strands of pikake. We watched the couples dance to "Ain't No Woman Like The One I Got." Jay did the Bump with Nina. Wesley held Monica close. Hoagie flirted with Miss Takata. Steve and Heidi made out beside a potted palm. A bearded man with a camera asked if we'd pose for a picture and Laura shook her head. She walked over to the buffet table and pulled a plate off the stack. She cut a slice of grasshopper pie and returned to our table. It felt as if everything I'd gained in my last semester at Punahou was nothing at all.

I walked over to Laura. "I need some air," I said,

"wanna come?"

Laura picked up a fork and cut the pie. "No."

I pushed open the glass door and my loafers squeaked across the redwood deck. Dots of red, green, yellow, and blue from the disco ball played over the slats. A three-quarter moon broke through the clouds and lit up the rolling meadows. I wrapped my hands around the cold steel railing. I felt like a fool. I was trying to erase years of being a nobody in these final weeks. I hated myself for using Laura. I looked toward the lot and saw my B-210 parked beside the lehua.

The glass door opened and Laura walked out. She leaned against the railing and looked up at the moon.

"I'm sorry," I told her.

"For what?"

"For rushing something that isn't there. We don't even know one other."

"Wanna split?" Laura asked.

"Do you?"

"Yes."

We danced one last song. Laura insisted. We slow danced to Cecilio and Kapono's "Lovin' In Your Eyes." The song was about romantic beginnings and learning not to hide love. The voices of The Lava Gods were soft and harmonic. Laura let me hold her close and I accidentally broke a strand of pikake. The flowers spilled like pearls over the floor.

"No biggie," Laura said.

*　　　*　　　*

We talked about college on the ride back to Palolo Valley. Laura was going to Lewis & Clark College in Portland. She wanted to become a surgeon so she could return to Seoul to help her people. Most of her relatives were still there. I parked outside her house and turned off the engine. She sat in the passenger seat looking straight ahead. I leaned over and kissed her on the cheek.

"Look, Jeff," Laura said, "mahalo for the prom, but our date's pau."

I put my arm around her and pulled her close. She turned her face and let me kiss her.

"Good thing you've got Hawaiian blood," Laura said.

"Why?"

"It's the only way I could convince Ma you had any redeeming qualities. But you know what?"

"What?"

"Your mother doesn't approve of me."

"You never met her."

"That time I phoned about Steinbeck, I heard it in her voice. She wants you with a haole girl."

"I think Ma wants you with a Korean boy."

"What's wrong with that?" she asked. "You're going to Boulder and I'm going to Portland."

"I'll be home for Christmas."

"Me too. And you'll have your haole girl and I'll have my Korean boy."

"Are there many Koreans in Portland?"

Laura laughed and toyed with her hair.

The bamboo porch light flicked off and on, off and on.

"That's Ma's signal," she said.

I walked Laura to the front door. Termites and moths swarmed the porch light and geckos were having a bug luau. The door flew open and Ma had her hands on her hips. " 'Bout time, Missy!"

"Bluff," a man said in the back room, "big bluff!"

"Hi, Ma," Laura said. She stood on the Astroturf and stepped out of her wedgees.

"Have good time?"

"Yes, Ma."

"Come inside," Ma told me. "But first, take off da shoe."

I took off my loafers, placed them on the Astroturf, and walked in.

"Ai-ya!" Pa said in the back room. Smoke hung in the doorway like a curtain.

"What wrong with Pa?" I asked.

Laura rolled her eyes. "He's swearing," she said, "as usual."

Ma nodded. "Lose big."

"How much is big?" I asked.

"Fifty dollah."

Laura peeked into the back room.

"How's my favorite daughta?" Pa asked.

"I'm your only daughter," Laura answered, "and don't smoke so much."

"Get hum ha poak and hoi sin chickin leftova," Ma

told me. "Which ya like?"

"I'll try the chicken," I said.

*   *   *

On the drive home I sang "Oahu`a." Then I sang the Punahou fight song. My voice was flat and off-key but it didn't matter. It started raining and I sang to the beat of the wiper blades. I thought about Laura leaving for Oregon. I imagined crossing paths with her at the airport and our parents being forced to meet. I wondered how Laura would handle it if that happened. I looked down at the hoi sin chicken over glass noodles—it was in the container that had once held Laura's corsage. Maybe this was a message from Ma to leave her daughter alone.

*   *   *

We received our diplomas at the HIC and our graduation party was at Dole Cafeteria. Students and faculty were whooping it up in the cafeteria when I got there. Hugh helped Lucy hang a class banner. A disco ball had been suspended from the ceiling on the Diamond Head side and "Crocodile Rock" played over the speakers. Grads danced fox trots and cha-cha-chas to the music, steps we'd all learned in mandatory dance class as freshmen. George fox trotted with Dawn. "Oh, I remember that!" said Monica as she cha-chaed with Speedy. Mr. Farley showed Miss Meyer how to do the Swim. Bouquets of blue and yellow balloons were tethered to the tables and chairs. Ben and Mike Swenson gobbled down hunks of blue and yellow sheet cake while a Twinkie spiked a bowl of Hawaiian Punch with booze from a hip flask. Wayne flirted with

Mindy over by the milk dispenser and I saw Steve outside kissing Heidi under the banyan tree. "Oahu`a" came on and Lucy helped everyone remember the lyrics.

I wandered over to a photo gallery on the Pearl Harbor side. The gallery spanned freshman to senior year and included candids from the prom. Jay and Coop were checking out pictures of them playing volleyball. I saw one of me and Laura taken during our slow dance and it seemed as if we were a couple.

"No ka oi of us," came a girl's voice, "don't you think?"

I turned around and saw Laura. She had on a lavender party dress with spaghetti straps and a puka shell necklace. The corsage I'd given her was around her wrist— it looked just as fresh as prom night. I sensed something different about her, a sadness in the eyes and a vulnerability in the way she held herself. Roberta Flack sang "Killing Me Softly With His Song" over the speakers.

"Wanna go outside, Laura?"

"Okay."

I pushed open the door and we walked down the stairs to middle field. The stars seemed closer that I'd ever seen them and the grass looked blue in the moonlight. We strolled over to Old School Hall and I plucked a plumeria off a tree and gave it to Laura. She put the flower behind her left ear and I took her in my arms and kissed her. This time she kissed me back. We kissed and hugged and kissed again.

"Know what?" she asked in the moonlight.

"What?"

"I'm sorry for being such a cold ahi on prom night."

"That's okay," I said.

"No, it's not. I realized something when I saw you tonight at graduation."

"Oh, yeah?"

"You're someone worth knowing, Jeff Gill," she said, "and I don't want to lose you."

GLOSSARY
OF WORDS AND PHRASES

WORDS:

ae: yes

ahi: tuna

aina: land

akamai: smart, clever

akua: ghost

aloha: hello, goodbye, and love

auwe: my goodness

blahlah: derogatory island slang for a Samoan man

bumboola: big marble

flip-flops: rubber slippers

hala: pandanus tree

hana: work

hanabuttah: phlegm

hanai: raised not by parents but by extended family

haole: white person

hapa haole: part Hawaiian and part white

hapai: pregnant

haupia: coconut pudding

hele: go

holoku: formal gown

hula: dance telling a story through gesture and pace

kahuna: witch doctor

kala: money

kama'aina: islander, local

kamani: large tree whose wood is used for calabashes

kanaka: person with Hawaiian blood

kapakahi: lopsided, crooked

kiawe: Algaroba tree known for its thorny branches

kini: marble

koa: strong lustrous wood used to make canoes

kua'aina: country bumpkin, idiot

kukae: excrement

kuku: thorny weed

kukui: candlenut tree

kulikuli: be quiet

ku'uipo: sweetheart

lauhala: leaf of the hala tree

lehua: flower or the tree itself

lei: garland of flowers

luau: party featuring a meal of fish, poi, and kalua pig

mahalo: thank you

mahimahi: best-tasting fish in island waters

mahu: gay

maile: twining shrub with fragrant leaves

makai: ocean side

makas: eyes

malahini: newcomer

manapua: steamed bun filled with pork and spices

mana'o: feeling, belief

manuahi: illegitimate

mauka: mountain side

moelepo: soft, lazy, shiftless

moke: local tough guy

mo'opuna: grandchild

okole: ass

ono: delicious

opihi: good-eating limpet

owama: baby goatfish

paipo: belly board

pakalaki: bad, unlucky

pakalolo: marijuana

palaka: blue and white checkered shirt

pau: finished

pikake: Arabian jasmine

pili: grass

pilikia: trouble

plumeria: fragrant island flower used for leis

poha: gooseberry

poi: pudding made by pounding the taro root

Portagee: Portuguese

puhi'u: fart

puka: hole

pune'e: big bed that doubles as a couch

pupu: hors d'oeuvre

pupule: crazy

taro: leafy green plant where poi comes from

ti: plant with narrow green or red leaves

talofa: derogatory island slang for Samoan or Tongan

tutu: grandmother

ulua: skipjack (fish)

wahine: girl or woman

PHRASES:

akua pololi: hungry ghosts

kanaka maoli: having at least 50% Hawaiian blood

Killahaole Day: day when locals beat up haoles

make moe'uhane: death dreams

Mo'o Ali'i: shark god

no ka oi: the best, great, everything's fine

'O'io Marchers: night-marching ghosts

okole kala: tightwad

ono for: craving

pa'a the waha: shut your mouth

pau hana: work's done

piha kanaka maoli: having pure Hawaiian ancestry

poi dog: dog of mixed breeds, mutt